REDWOOD LIBRARY

NEWPORT, R. I.

WITHDRAWN

Arabic Short Stories

Arabic Short Stories

Translated by
Denys Johnson-Davies

Quartet Books
London Melbourne New York

First published by Quartet Books Limited 1983
A member of the Namara Group
27/29 Goodge Street, London W1P 1FD

Reprinted 1983

Copyright © 1983 by Denys Johnson-Davies

British Library Cataloguing in Publication Data

Arabic short stories.
  1. Short stories, Arabic—Translations into English
  2. Short stories, English—Translations from Arabic
  I. Johnson-Davies, Denys
  892'.7301'08[FS]   PJ7694.E8

ISBN 0-7043-2367-2

Phototypeset by MC Typeset, Chatham, Kent
Printed in Great Britain
by Nene Litho and bound by Woolnough Bookbinders
both of Wellingborough, Northants

CONTENTS

MAR 1 6 1994

NOTES ON AUTHORS

Yusuf Idris was born in 1927 in a village in the Delta of Egypt. He was first induced to write not so much through the influence of any particular author, Arab or foreign, as by his feeling that the Egyptian stories he read as a boy were inadequate to the reality around him. In 1954 his first collection of short stories, with an introduction by the eminent scholar Taha Hussein, established him as a writer of unique talent. He had in the meantime become qualified as a doctor, and his experiences, in private practice and as a government health inspector, have provided him with much of his material. He later became influenced by his readings of Gorki and then of Chekhov; he also acknowledges a debt to the detective story and to *The Thousand and One·Nights* and other folk literature. A political consciousness and a concern with the underprivileged underlie both his short stories and his plays. His work has been translated into most major languages. A volume of his stories is available in the 'Arab Authors' series and a book containing three of his longer stories is shortly to be added to the series.

Ibrahim Ishaq Ibrahim was born in 1946 in the province of Eastern Darfour in the Sudan. He studied in Omdurman, then taught English language and literature at various secondary schools, also Islamic culture at the University of Omdurman. He has published a number of studies on modern Sudanese literature and has a special interest in folklore about which he has written extensively. His creative writings, including three novels, deal mainly with village life in Darfour. He is at present teaching English at an intermediate school in Riyadh. Saudi Arabia.

Mohamed El-Bisatie was born in 1938 and works as a government official; at present he is seconded to the Saudi Arabian government and works in Riyadh. He has published three volumes of short stories, a novel and two novellas published in a single volume.

Mohammed Ahmed Abdul Wali was a Yemeni writer who published several books of short stories and novels in Beirut. He lived much of his life abroad, in particular in Leningrad. It is believed that he met his death in an air crash at Sanaa in the early seventies.

Mohammed Khudayyir was born and lives in southern Iraq near Basra where he works as a schoolteacher. Though he has published only two volumes of short stories, *The Black Kingdom* and *At a Temperature of 45 Centigrade*, he is one of the most original talents writing in the Arab world today.

Bahaa Taher was born at Giza, on the outskirts of Cairo of a family originally from Karnak in Upper Egypt. After taking a degree in history at Cairo University he started working on the cultural programme of Cairo radio, of which he later became the deputy-director. He produced a great variety of plays ranging from the Greek dramatists to works by Samuel Beckett. For some years he was theatre critic to one of Cairo's leading literary magazines, but it is as a writer of short stories that he is best known. He has, however, published only one small volume, in 1972. Since 1981 he has been working as a translator in the Arabic section of the United Nations in Geneva.

Yusuf Sharouni was born in 1924 in the Delta of Egypt. He studied philosophy at Cairo University and worked for a time as a teacher in the Sudan. He presently holds a senior position in the Supreme Council for the Arts, Literature and Social Sciences in Cairo. His creative writing is confined to the short story of which he is one of the Arab world's leading practitioners. He has also published several volumes of literary criticism.

Alifa Rifaat is in her early fifties and lives in Cairo with her children. The widow of a police officer, she spent most of her married life in different parts of the Egyptian countryside and it is largely from these years that she draws the material for her short stories, of which she has published two volumes. The story by which she is here represented has been broadcast on BBC Radio 3. A volume of her stories in translation is shortly to appear under the imprint of Quartet Books.

Tayeb Salih was born in 1929 in a village in the north of the Sudan, the setting for most of his writings. After studying at Khartoum University, he came to England and continued his studies at Exeter University. Much of his working life was spent in London with the BBC Arabic service. He later went to Qatar in the Arabian Gulf as Director-General of Information and is now employed with Unesco in Paris. The story by which he is here represented first appeared in *Encounter*. Two short novels, *The Wedding of Zein* and *Season of Migration to the North* have been published in one volume by Quartet Books. His last two works of fiction, two novellas, are to appear together under the Onyx Press imprint in a Unesco-sponsored translation. His writings have been widely translated.

Ibrahim Al-Kouni was born in 1948 in Ghadames, Libya. He graduated from the Gorki Institute in Moscow and is now in charge of the Libyan People's Bureau in Warsaw. He has published a volume of short stories, also books of essays and criticism.

Nabil Gorgy, born in Cairo in 1944, studied civil engineering at Cairo University and later worked as an engineer in and around New York. He has now returned to live in Cairo and occupies himself with writing and running his own art gallery. He is widely read in Egyptology, mythology and mysticism, including Sufism. A few of his short stories, also a short mystical novel entitled *The Door*, have been published. He has recently completed another novel.

Hanan Shaykh comes from southern Lebanon but lived most of her early life in Beirut. She attended the American College for Girls in Cairo where, at the age of twenty-one, she wrote her first novel. Returning to Beirut, she worked on a women's magazine and for the literary supplement of the leading daily paper. With marriage, she moved with her husband to the Arabian Gulf, where she lived for several years and wrote her second novel. Her third novel, *The Story of Zahra*, was written largely in London, where she has a home, and is presently being translated into English. The story here included has been taken from her recently published volume of short stories entitled *Desert Rose*.

Abdul Ilah Abdul Razzak was born in Basra, Iraq, in 1939. He studied Arabic literature and graduated from Baghdad University in 1964. He has published two volumes of short stories and also writes criticism of modern Arabic literature.

Edward El-Kharrat was born in 1926 in Alexandria. He read law at Alexandria University and worked in a variety of jobs, including that of storehouse assistant at the Royal Navy Victualling Department. Since 1959 he has been with the Afro-Asian Peoples' Solidarity Organization and the Afro-Asian Writers' Association of which he is now the Deputy Secretary-General. His first book of short stories, *High Walls*, was published at his own expense in 1959; despite meagre sales it has had considerable influence on the Egyptian short story. His preoccupation with language and a convoluted style reminiscent of Proust present special difficulties to the translator. He himself has translated widely from English and French. A second book of short stories, *Hours of Pride*, came out in 1972, and a highly-praised novel, *Rama and the Dragon*, in 1979. He has written about and encouraged younger generations of writers.

Mohammed Barrada was born in Rabat, Morocco, in 1938. He took a degree in Arabic from Cairo University and a doctorate from Paris in modern literary criticism. He has published a number of critical works and has translated books from the French. A volume of his short stories was published in Beirut in 1979. He is presently Professor of Arabic at the University in Rabat and President of the Union of Moroccan Writers.

Yusuf Abu Rayya was born in 1955 in a village near the town of Zagazig. He studied journalism at Cairo University and works as a government servant, also as a journalist, in Cairo. He has published his stories in magazines in Egypt and the Arab countries but has not collected any of them into a volume.

Abdel-Hakim Kassem was born in 1935. He went to school in Tanta and to Alexandria University. He became politically active and in 1967 was sentenced to five years' imprisonment by a military court. On coming out of prison he published his well-known novel *The Seven Days of Man*. He has published several other short novels, also a number of short stories. For the past few years he has been living in Berlin.

Mohammed Chukri was born in 1935 in the region of Nadhor in northern Morocco and for most of his life has lived in Tangier. For a number of years he earned his living as a teacher but is now employed as cultural adviser to an international radio station. Peter Owen has published a number of translations of his writings made by the American novelist Paul Bowles, including an autobiography *For Bread Alone* and *Jean Genet in Tangier*. Much of his writing remains in manuscript owing to his inability to find a publisher in the Arab world willing to print such outspoken material. Recently a volume of his stories, under the title of the story here presented, was published in Beirut. Until the age of twenty-one he had not known how to read or write.

Gamil Atia Ibrahim was born in Cairo in 1937. After taking his degree at the Faculty of Commerce, he changed his career and took a diploma in art appreciation at the Academy of Arts and worked with the Ministry of Culture. He was recently given an MA for a thesis on prehistoric art in Africa. For two years he taught in northern Morocco and his novel *Asila*, published in Damascus in 1980, draws on this experience. A volume of his short stories was published in Baghdad in 1977. He presently lives in Basle – he is married to a Swiss – and works as a correspondent for several Arabic publications.

Habib Selmi was born in a Tunisian village in 1951. He obtained his degree from the University of Tunis in Arabic literature and then taught for five years in secondary schools. He now works full-time as a writer and journalist for Tunisian and other Arabic papers, including an Arabic magazine published in Paris. He received a state prize for a work of fiction that appeared in 1978. Recently he has translated a number of short stories by Gabriel Garcia Marquez.

Ibrahim Aslan was born in 1939. He did not complete his secondary education and is largely self-educated. After being employed in a variety of jobs, he now works as a government employee in wireless communications in Cairo. Despite the fact that he has published only one volume of short stories, *The Lake of Evening*, he is regarded as one of Egypt's most talented writers. A novel on which he has been working for many years entitled *The Heron* is shortly to be published in Beirut. A further volume of short stories is also due out.

Zakaria Tamer was born in Damascus in 1929. With little formal education, he has established himself, through four volumes of short stories, as one of the best-known exponents of the short story in the Arab world. His stories, written in a distinctive and uncluttered style, are often allegorical with political overtones. His writings for children enjoy great success. In Damascus he held various governmental posts before coming to work on one of the Arabic papers produced in London. He recently left for Kuwait to advise on the publication of children's books.

Ghassan Kanafani was born in Acre, Palestine, in 1936 and was killed in Beirut in 1972 when his car was booby-trapped. Before moving to Beirut, where he worked as spokesman for the Popular Front for the Liberation of Palestine, he taught and worked as a journalist in Damascus and Kuwait; it is the latter country that provides the background for the story by which he is here represented. Though deeply involved in politics he found the time to become the leading Palestinian prose-writer. He published five novels and five collections of short stories, also studies of Palestinian literature. His best-known novel, *Men in the Sun*, together with several short stories, is available in the 'Arab Authors' series.

Mahmoud Al-Wardani was born in 1950. A small volume of his stories was published in Cairo in 1982; a further volume is shortly to appear under the imprint of the General Egyptian Book Organization in Cairo.

YUSUF IDRIS

The Chair Carrier

You can believe it or not, but excuse me for saying that your opinion is of no concern at all to me. It's enough for me that I saw him, met him, talked to him and observed the chair with my own eyes. Thus I considered that I had been witness to a miracle. But even more miraculous – indeed more disastrous – was that neither the man, the chair, nor the incident caused a single passer-by in Opera Square, in Gumhouriyya Street, or in Cairo – or maybe in the whole wide world – to come to a stop at that moment.

It was a vast chair. Looking at it you'd think it had come from some other world, or that it had been constructed for some festival, such a colossal chair, as though it were an institution all on its own, its seat immense and softly covered with leopard skin and silken cushions. Once you'd seen it your great dream was to sit in it, be it just the once, just for a moment. A moving chair, it moved forward with stately gait as though it were in some religious procession. You'd think it was moving of its own accord. In awe and amazement you almost prostrated yourself before it in worship and offered up sacrifices to it.

Eventually, however, I made out, between the four massive legs that ended in glistening gilded hooves, a fifth leg. It was skinny and looked strange amidst all that bulk and splendour; it was, though, no leg but a thin, gaunt human being upon whose body the sweat had formed runnels and rivulets and had caused woods and groves of hair to sprout. Believe me, by all that's holy, I'm neither lying nor exaggerating, simply relating, be it ever so inadequately, what I saw. How was it that such a thin, frail man was carrying a chair like this one, a chair that weighed at least a ton, and maybe several? That was the proposition that was presented to one's mind – it was like some conjuring trick. But you had only to look longer and more closely to find that there was no deception, that the man really was carrying the chair all on his own and moving along with it.

What was even more extraordinary and more weird, something that was truly alarming, was that none of the passers-by in Opera Square, in Gumhouriyya Street or maybe in the whole of Cairo, was at all astonished or treated the matter as if it was anything untoward, but rather as something quite normal and unremarkable, as if the chair were as light as a butterfly and was being carried around by a young lad. I looked at the people and at the chair and at the man, thinking that I would spot the raising of an eyebrow, or lips sucked back in alarm, or hear a cry of amazement, but there was absolutely no reaction.

I began to feel that the whole thing was too ghastly to contemplate any longer. At this very moment the man with his burden was no more than a step or two away from me and I was able to see his good-natured face, despite its many wrinkles. Even so it was impossible to determine his age. I then saw something more about him: he was naked except for a stout waistband from which hung, in front and behind, a covering made of sailcloth. Yet you would surely have to come to a stop, conscious that your mind had, like an empty room, begun to set off echoes telling you that, dressed as he was, he was a stranger not only to Cairo but to our whole era. You had the sensation of having seen his like in books about history or archaeology. And so I was surprised by the smile he gave, the kind of meek smile a beggar gives, and by a voice that mouthed words:

'May God have mercy on your parents, my son. You wouldn't have seen Uncle Ptah Ra'?'

Was he speaking hieroglyphics pronounced as Arabic, or Arabic pronounced as hieroglyphics? Could the man be an ancient Egyptian? I rounded on him:

'Listen here – don't start telling me you're an ancient Egyptian?'

'And are there ancient and modern? I'm simply an Egyptian.'

'And what's this chair?'

'It's what I'm carrying. Why do you think I'm going around looking for Uncle Ptah Ra'? It's so that he may order me to put it down just as he ordered me to carry it. I'm done in.'

'You've been carrying it for long?'

'For a very long time, you can't imagine.'

'A year?'

'What do you mean by a year, my son? Tell anyone who asks –
a year and then a few thousand.'

'Thousand what?'

'Years.'

'From the time of the Pyramids, for example?'

'From before that. From the time of the Nile.'

'What do you mean: from the time of the Nile?'

'From the time when the Nile wasn't called the Nile, and they
moved the capital from the mountain to the river bank, Uncle
Ptah brought me along and said "Porter, take it up". I took it up
and ever since I've been wandering all over the place looking for
him to tell me to put it down, but from that day to this I've not
found him.'

All ability or inclination to feel astonishment had completely
ended for me. Anyone capable of carrying a chair of such
dimensions and weight for a single moment could equally have
been carrying it for thousands of years. There was no occasion
for surprise or protest; all that was required was a question:

'And suppose you don't find Uncle Ptah Ra', are you going to
go on carrying it around?'

'What else shall I do? I'm carrying it and it's been deposited in
trust with me. I was ordered to carry it, so how can I put it down
without being ordered to?'

Perhaps it was anger that made me say: 'Put it down. Aren't
you fed up, man? Aren't you tired? Throw it away, break it up,
burn it. Chairs are made to carry people, not for people to carry
them.'

'I can't. Do you think I'm carrying it for fun? I'm carrying it
because that's the way I earn my living.'

'So what? Seeing that it's wearing you out and breaking your
back, you should throw it down – you should have done so
ages ago.'

'That's how you look at things because you're safely out of it;
you're not carrying it, so you don't care. I'm carrying it and it's
been deposited in trust with me, so I'm responsible for it.'

3

'Until when, for God's sake?'

'Till the order comes from Ptah Ra'.'

'He couldn't be more dead.'

'Then from his successor, his deputy, from one of his descendants, from anyone with a token of authorization from him.'

'All right then, I'm ordering you right now to put it down.'

'Your order will be obeyed – and thank you for your kindness – but are you related to him?'

'Unfortunately not.'

'Do you have a token of authorization from him?'

'No, I don't.'

'Then allow me to be on my way.'

He had begun to move off, but I shouted out to him to stop, for I had noticed something that looked like an announcement or sign fixed to the front of the chair. In actual fact it was a piece of gazelle-hide with ancient writing on it, looking as though it was from the earliest copies of the Revealed Books. It was with difficulty that I read:

> O chair carrier,
> You have carried enough
> And the time has come for you to be carried in a chair.
> This great chair,
> The like of which has not been made,
> Is for you alone.
> Carry it
> And take it to your home.
> Put it in the place of honour
> And seat yourself upon it your whole life long.
> And when you die
> It shall belong to your sons.

'This, Mr Chair Carrier, is the order of Ptah Ra', an order that is precise and was issued at the same moment in which he ordered you to carry the chair. It is sealed with his signature and cartouche.'

All this I told him with great joy, a joy that exploded as from someone who had been almost stifled. Ever since I had seen the chair and known the story I had felt as though it were I who was

4

carrying it and had done so for thousands of years; it was as though it were my back that was being broken, and as though the joy that now came to me were my own joy at being released at long last.

The man listened to me with head lowered, without a tremor of emotion: just waited with head lowered for me to finish, and no sooner had I done so than he raised his head. I had been expecting a joy similar to my own, even an expression of delight, but I found no reaction.

'The order's written right there above your head – written ages ago.'

'But I don't know how to read.'

'But I've just read it out to you.'

'I'll believe it only if there's a token of authorization. Have you such a token?'

When I made no reply he muttered angrily as he turned away:

'All I get from you people is obstruction. Man, it's a heavy load and the day's scarcely long enough for making just the one round.'

I stood watching him. The chair had started to move at its slow, steady pace, making one think that it moved by itself. Once again the man had become its thin fifth leg, capable on its own of setting it in motion.

I stood watching him as he moved away, panting and groaning and with the sweat pouring off him.

I stood there at a loss, asking myself whether I shouldn't catch him up and kill him and thus give vent to my exasperation. Should I rush forward and topple the chair forcibly from his shoulders and make him take a rest? Or should I content myself with the sensation of enraged irritation I had for him? Or should I calm down and feel sorry for him?

Or should I blame myself for not knowing what the token of authorization was?

IBRAHIM ISHAQ IBRAHIM

The Gap in Kaltouma's Fence

On my return last time from the city I found that squat, fair-skinned man with the handsome features in Kaltouma's yard. It was as though he owned the place, while Kaltouma behaved as if, by chance, she had become oblivious of her notorious bad humour, had cast it off from herself, had broken through it and become all new and pleasant and charming as I'd never seen her before. At a loss about the man, I asked Sittana's people at our house:

'Who would he be?'

'The Faki[1] al-Baseer.'

'And what would he be doing in Kaltouma's house?'

Sittana gave me an enquiring look that was clearly disapproving.

'Hey, boy, what's this "what would he be doing"? Can't a man be in his own home?'

I think that I myself began to stare at Sittana's face with disapproving questioning till Umm al-Fadl interrupted me gently, stressing her words with casual ease:

'Hey, listen here to me, that man's Kaltouma's husband. They got married two months ago. He's a polite and educated man but very strict and proper.'

'Kaltouma got married after all that time?'

This time Sittana interrupted me, her voice raised in annoyance:

'And what's wrong with that? Just tell me what's wrong?'

I exchanged glances of disbelief with her and Umm al-Fadl till the latter said to me:

'When you address him, say "Uncle Abdul Maula", or you can "Sayyidna al-Baseer". That would be right and correct.'

I looked at the two of them and, strangely enough, I began to take it in. So I must ask in order to know exactly what had occurred whereby Kaltouma had got herself married. It meant asking once and for all, however difficult it might be, for I too am of the Kabashi and must know what took place. If I'm not entitled to know, then who is?

I knew myself to be upset for later I came to understand within myself that I had known Kaltouma only in her days of terrible uncouthness of manner. It was as though I had taken it for granted that she could never be like Sittana or Umm al-Fadl; it was as though I'd placed her with my uncle Abdul Qadir and Omar on one and the same footing. This was something of long standing, though it doesn't really require someone as stupid as I to think of her as being innately like that. Some people say she was born headstrong and with a heart of stone, and most of the Kabashis regard her as having acquired this severity of character from having lived with my grandfather al-Nu'man, it being known amongst us that my grandfather al-Nu'man was her uncle, the son of her father's uncle, and that he had married her when she was still young. Among the branches and roots of the Kabashi clan they recall the time when he was as famous as my grandfather Fadeelou, although they claim he was a solid, rational man unlike my grandfather Fadeelou. My grandfather al-Nu'man had died in Kharubat and Kaltouma had come with Abdul Qadir, also with Omar's people, and they had later on settled in Dikka because of the cattle. Sheikh Adam Mehaireeqa had asked for her in marriage but she had refused him. Some women at the village called her mad and Umm al-Fadl went so far as to curse them openly. She, together with Sittana, told them they didn't know how to rate men and that my grandfather al-Nu'man was worth exactly ten of someone like Sheikh Adam, and even of the Shartay[2] himself and that were they to collect all the Shartays of the region from one end to the other they wouldn't be worth the ground he sat on. These were some of the stormy and amusing happenings that took place in the days when we were not yet born. Even the Shartay was extremely indignant at the mothers' words and he expounded what they had said to Omar's and Abdul Qadir's group of men. For the second time those men said to him: 'They were only telling the truth.' The

Shartay got into a tearing rage which he kept up for a whole year and from which the Children of Kabashi suffered horribly.

'This Faki al-Baseer,' I said to Umm Ajab in her house, 'where's he come from?'

She related to me everything she knew. She said to me: 'Kaltouma – what a person she is!' I confirmed this to her: Kaltouma's not only difficult, she's bright too. It was as though she'd absorbed knowledge about people and the way people think from my grandfather al-Nu'man with the whole of her body, and Umm al-Ajab assured me that that man was learned and his courage not inconsiderable, also that she herself had told Kaltouma that the words of all those people wouldn't go to waste. The yard of a young woman like Kaltouma certainly shouldn't lie empty; to them it looked like a crack in a water trough. The first man who had protected her honour had died when his time had come and she had been left to her fate and to look around for another man to protect her. It was as though Kaltouma, when looking at men, didn't find anyone to match up to my grandfather al-Nu'man, and that, in despair, she no longer troubled about men. I thought for a moment that were I able to find sufficient resolve I would go and ask Kaltouma herself, but for the fact that Sittana had scared me by saying that that man – exactly as I had heard inside the yard – had now become an object of great esteem for Omar and Abdul Qadir and was beloved of uncles and neighbours.

Sittana laughed as she recounted to me how he had come one morning to her door, standing there and knocking. Omar had got up and gone to him, with Sittana listening to the two of them. Omar had taken him along to the grass shelter and she had heard them exchanging short, incisive words and she had feared that something had occurred. When the two of them had gone out she didn't waste any time but went off at a run to find out the news from Kaltouma. Kaltouma did no more than smile gently and pat Sittana on the shoulder. Sittana listened in at Abdul Qadir's house and heard the voices of Omar and the man with Abdul Qadir delivering themselves of such deliberate and serious talk that her heart beat with fear, while Kaltouma did no more than give that inscrutable smile of hers so that Sittana came to suspect that she didn't have a heart and that her feelings had petrified into a cruel indifference towards things both remote and close. There came to them, in Abdul Qadir's house, the voices of Hajj Ahmed, Faki Mahmoud, the maternal uncle of Umm Ajab's son and Basous, while Sittana's heart, she told me, was fluttering like a feather. Kaltouma the while was still merely smiling until shrieks of joy were heard to issue forth from Abdul Qadir's yard, which caused Sittana to breathe a sigh of relief. Laughing, she said to me:

'Kaltouma's an enemy, an enemy. She absolutely refused to let me in to what was going on, just sitting there and looking down and laughing. And so it went on till I came home and Omar came along and said to me: "By the way, we've married Kaltouma off to that Faki who's staying at Ahmed's place." '

My uncle Abdul Qadir informed me of other things. One day I was with Mun'im in Hajj Ahmed's house and he took me to the place in the yard which divides off their house from Kaltouma's. We returned to the grass shelter and he started right away putting me in the picture. The Faki used to sit mornings and evenings around there writing out Qur'anic charms for Hanouna. During the time of the wedding the women discovered that opening between the two yards both for going in by and coming out through, and thereafter it remained open. The Faki was writing away and Kaltouma, without noticing him, came and bent down to pass through the gap in the fence and was surprised to find the Faki in front of her as she was halfway through the opening, one foot in her own yard and one in Hajj Ahmed's, not knowing whether to retreat or to continue on, while the Faki, surrounded by his wooden tablets and aware of her hesitation, refrained from looking at her. Like someone rooted to the spot she remained in the gap. I knew this deep inside of me but I didn't tell Mun'im. She was arguing in her heart about the appropriate action to be taken: the childish (as she saw it) act of making her escape by running off like some young virgin back to her house, or to continue on and enter, for – when all was said and done – she was no more than an elderly woman, though not sufficiently covered up to come striding along in the presence of strangers. All the while the Faki was averting his gaze, then, becoming embarrassed at not knowing why she was staying on there, neither coming nor going, he forgot about his writing and his wooden tablets, for no man possesses two hearts, while the mind – as the teacher says – only performs its function by concentrating on something and disregarding the existence of all other distractions.

Mun'im told me that Kaltouma didn't move and waited, while the Faki, in a state of embarrassment, did not raise his head. Kaltouma, too, pretended to pay no attention to him and didn't call out for fear of the seductiveness of the female voice. As good luck would have it, Hanouna's mother appeared from the kitchen, saw Kaltouma and ran to her. They whispered together, then Hanouna's mother rushed off and came back with an outer garment with which to cover up Kaltouma properly, and the two of them went inside.

The following day, right early in the morning, Kaltouma blocked up that gap, building it up with sturdy reeds so that it looked as if there'd never been a hole there. Hanouna said to Mun'im that when the Faki sat down to write in the forenoon he was, for a time, at a loss to write a thing, having seen that the opening to that building had been blocked off from the opposite side. He bent over and wrote until the sun rose up, then he put aside the tablets and went off to the *souk*. Hanouna said she heard him mumbling at the door: 'Praise be to Thee, O Lord, the Manipulator of hearts.' When he returned at noon he wrote for a while and called out to Hanouna's mother to ask her whether that woman had a husband and why it was that the Hajj had let her open up a gap through to his house. Hanouna's mother informed him that she was unmarried, saying that the woman's husband had died some time ago. The Faki then asked Hanouna's mother what had made Kaltouma stop for such a long time at the gap and she told him she was waiting for an outer garment. Hanouna's mother spoke at length and mentioned to the Faki how Kaltouma hadn't known yesterday whether to regard herself as an elderly woman who had passed the change of life, or whether she should run away, which would have meant that she was playing at being young when, as she herself said, she was nothing but an old woman. The Faki had interrupted her:

'But she's not old at all, that one. If she said so, then she's an utter liar. She's a well-behaved woman, the daughter of good folk.'

Hanouna's mother had laughed and during the afternoon she had informed Kaltouma, who became so furious she almost burst. Hanouna's mother made fun of her, telling her that she was scared of men to such an extent that she could not even accept it being said about her that she hadn't yet passed the time of life when a woman is still young and vigorous of spirit, and that she should know that she had every right to make herself up and enjoy herself and be true to her real self again one day.

Umm Ajab made things even clearer for me by stating how many times Kaltouma had thought of reviling the Faki and complaining of him to Omar. The important thing for her was to do something in relation to him, but instead she stayed at home with her thoughts. On the last day Hanouna's mother asked her why it was, then, that she had closed up the opening between the two of them. Kaltouma had stammered; then, when her neighbour had laughed, she had been emboldened by annoyance to explain to her:

'All men are the same, and there's no assurance in the way they look at one. There's evil in looking. I did what I had to do. I'm the daughter of the saintly Sheikh and the widow of the late al-Nu'man. Let me sit at home. If what prompts that man isn't just the Devil, if he's really a good man, he shouldn't expect to see me through gaps in fences at the back of rear lanes. Let him do the right and open thing and come along by the front lane under the gaze of everyone. That's if he means well, sister. But if he just goes on saying things about me, by the name of my saintly grandfather he'll be hearing himself cursed throughout the village. My brothers are at hand and if they got enraged by what he says, he'd find no place to give him safety.'

It seems that the Faki had learned from the Hajj's wife what Kaltouma had said (Sittana said: 'Allah bless Hanouna's mother'), so he didn't write any charms for Hanouna that day either. Going out to the *souk*, he chatted with Abdul Raheem Basous and Hajj Ahmed and traced back the ancestry of his clan to the two of them, his roots showing that he was from the Sulaymania tribe on his father's side, while his mother was from Kinana, and he gave the two of them assurances that he was a man of uprightness. In the evening Basous and the Hajj met up with Omar and Abdul Qadir and they informed the two of them of the state the man was in, saying that it could be seen from his face that he was a decent man, also one of learning and refinement whose family background was well known, so what more did they ask for? Besides which, his intentions were of the best. They said to them that maybe the time had come for Kaltouma to listen to what her legal guardians had to say and to comply with it, instead of their giving in to her every wish, even when there were imperative reasons not to, rather than sit around amidst the clans solitary and unmarried. If one day or night some catastrophe were to befall the people no one would be waiting for some man of substance to emerge from her compound; there would only be herself to take up her axe and fight alongside the men, and this would avail nothing. It seems that Omar and Abdul Qadir felt for the first time, after the telling off they'd had from Basous and the Hajj, the extent to which they had neglected the interests of Kaltouma who had all along remained arrogant and obdurate.

They asked of Hajj Ahmed that the Faki should meet the two of them first thing in the morning at their houses. And so it happened. They didn't ask Kaltouma (they knew from the Hajj through his wife about what she'd said) and no one paid any attention to the opinion she might express openly. The men gathered at Abdul Qadir's and they brought her back a married woman. During the day they emitted shrieks of joy and in the evening they took the radiant and resolute Faki into the compound as lord and master.

I am surprised at my uncle Abdul Qadir, and it's as though I still do not believe that Kaltouma will go back to being like Sittana, Umm al-Fadl and the other women, gentle and compliant. It is as if the whole transformation had come about suddenly owing to the fact that the Faki al-Baseer, as by a miracle, had made of my grandfather someone who counted for no more than anyone else from the Kabashi clan, so famed for intelligence, knowledge and wisdom. He had married and died and nothing remained of him but a memory.

Notes
1. A Faki is a man learned in religious law.
2. A Shartay is a tribal chief in the western district of Darfour in the Sudan.

12

MOHAMED EL-BISATIE

My Brother

Behind the house the ground sloped down slightly to the canal bank. Round it were remnants of a mud wall. One of its corners still stood intact on the bank and when the canal waters went down I could see it from the other bank looking as if it had increased in height. The part hidden in the water would come into view, greatly wasted away, its stonework blackened and with moss growing in it. On the side where the broken-down wall extended to, there were three date palms. One of them, the one closest to the house, had become curved. This was all that had happened throughout those years.

At night I would hear the rustling of their dried-up fronds on the window of his room, though this no longer worried me. The few dates that appeared at the end of their stalks would dry before ripening and all too soon would fall and the stalks would hang down empty for the whole season.

The lower part of the wall of the house bulged outwards, its stonework denuded of any crust of paint. With the passage of time it had begun to flake away and hollows began to make their appearance in the wall where the chickens would nest out of the rain.

In winter small plants would sprout between the date palms and alongside the wall of the house. Then, when winter ended, they would disappear.

Each time I crossed over by the wooden bridge to the other bank of the canal I would turn round to take a look at the house in the first light of early morning. I would see the two of them, my mother and my brother; their faces would be pressed against the

13

narrow back window as they stared out at me, silently laughing. My mother would stretch out her arm and point to me as I walked along the other bank.

On my return from the shop at noon I would again see them at the window, his enormous arm round her shoulders, and they'd stare out at me as I crossed the bridge.

Sometimes I'd not find them at the window. That would occur when I passed by the house carrying parcels of food. I would hear my mother's singing coming from within. In the hall in the space by the final flight of stairs I'd see him naked, his vast body filling the whole of a basin. He would squat down on one knee, gripping the rim with both hands. He would push it in a half-circle, then bring it back again, and my mother would pass around him, her body hunched up and the black headscarf wrapped round her head. She'd begin massaging his body as she sang in a low voice:
'Sayyid, O Abu Seed,
Sayyid, little sweet one.'
Suddenly he'd stop playing with the water and lower his head in attention, his twisted mouth lolling open. It would fill with saliva, his body would make a convulsive movement, and he'd give a fierce grunting sound:
'Ugh . . . Ugh . . .'
Thick hair covered his neck and hefty shoulders, spreading out more sparsely over his back and stomach. As I passed in front of the two of them, it would seem as if he hadn't seen me and he'd continue splashing the water round himself.

Every day he would have a bath in cold water. When the time came for his bath, just a little before noon, he'd look all about him and walk through the rooms and search in all the corners. Having found the basin, the lines of his face would relax and he'd carry it off to the middle of the hallway, remove his clothes and feel all over his naked body, as though seeing it for the first time. He'd grunt loudly:
'Ugh . . . Ugh . . .'
My mother would come at his call.
'Abu Seed wants to have a bath? Is that what it's about?'

During the day he'd sit on a white sheepskin rug inside the room in which the two of them slept. Her reddened, swollen hands would be lying in her lap, her face motionless, her lips pursed in a deep silence, and sometimes she would have closed her tired eyes and dozed off with her head against the wall.

She would be waiting for him to wake up.

At such moments the house was quiet, without a sound except for that of his snoring in the dark room. The neighbours had stopped coming ever since he began to wander round the house naked.

My mother would draw up a low chair and climb on to it so as to be able to look out of the window. She had a frail body and her face had grown very haggard and lined. Sometimes she would talk of pains in her hands and legs, though she was still capable of running with him round the table in the hallway.

When he was angry she would rush about screaming and clapping her hands and, with her black *galabia* raised, give little quivering leaps, like a hen drenched with water, and would sway about and begin to sing.

Snorting, he would take himself off, and my mother would follow him. He would turn, then circle round her for a while, rocking his vast body back and forth and staring at her over his shoulder and letting forth short grunts that were more like a rattling in the throat.

He would come to my room when the window was open and the space in front of it flooded in sunlight. He would sit motionless, his legs stretched out, his head on his chest. His pallid face would quiver, the cheeks quickly redden, then his long black eyelashes would close.

As the sun's rays shifted he would crawl after them. When they reached halfway across the room and had begun to withdraw, he would place his feet on the two sides of the patch of light and regard it in silence till it disappeared. Then he would get up and, on reaching the door, would turn round sullenly and look at me, grunting a little, then go out.

In front of the house there stretched a small track. My father had made it as a means of access to the garden. Having broken up the ground, he had surrounded it with thin wire fixed to supports made from the branches of trees. Even so, the goats would creep in from under the wire, attracted by the green leaves that had sprung up between the furrows.

At his death there were several bushes that had grown up on both sides of the tracks and my brother would rush out of the house to hide among them.

At the beginning, overcome by anxiety, my mother would dangle the pressure lamp from the window. He was still small and would slip in among the bushes and stretch himself out, twisting their thin stems on top of him so that they hid him. Each time I would think that he was bound to change his hiding-place; however, he continued to hide among them till in the end they were trampled down.

That was a relief to me. I always saw them as something strange in front of the house. They would remind me of that small garden my father had wanted to have.

My mother would say:

'Sayyid your brother – why don't you take him for a little walk?'

He would be standing behind her, clasping the end of her *galabia*. He was a thin boy with a long neck and large black eyes.

We would wait till nightfall and my mother would comb out his hair, arranging it to one side with a small curl on the forehead as he always liked best, and she would put a scarf round his neck and fasten it with a pin. Then, having dried his mouth, she would follow us to the steps with the pressure lamp.

Once outside the front door I would find that she had turned to the window, the lamp dangling from her hand, and by the time we had reached the canal she would have moved to the back window.

The light spread out in front of us as we crossed the bridge to the other bank.

We would make our way, his limp hand in my grasp, between the fields along a narrow lane that twisted and turned between areas of cultivation. The hill would come into view before us in

16

the sky's wan light. It was a small hill with some thickly-branched trees around it. Letting go of my hand, he would dash off to climb the hill and I would lie down and listen to the sounds of carts passing along the dirt track. I would hear the sound of his grunts from where he had squatted down at the top of the hill. Then I'd hear them close at hand as he crept up stealthily on me so as to jump on to my shoulders. When the mulberry trees were in fruit I would go down to the nearby trees and would move with him from tree to tree. He would grasp hold of a branch and raise himself up slightly on my shoulders. When he'd finished with it he'd swing his legs against my chest and I'd move off to another branch.

He would eat greedily and quickly grew to a large size.

Occasionally he would doze off as we were taking our supper and my mother would sign to me and I'd carry him to his bed. There she would press down on his cheeks and put her finger into his mouth to empty it of rice.

Days would pass during which I wouldn't see him; this was when I would return late from the shop. Maybe I'd see him without being aware of doing so. Then I'd be taken by surprise at how much larger he'd grown.

On our return he would remain on my shoulders. When the croaking of the frogs grew loud around us, he would stretch out his hand with a cloth bag and each time I would wonder how he'd managed to cram it into his pocket before we'd gone out.

He would lean over the canal bank, following the croaking as it rose and fell and would catch two or three. His hand with the bag would hang down alongside my shoulder.

I would remain on the watch for movements of his hands. Even so, directly we arrived, he'd empty out the bag, and in the light of the pressure lamp held by my mother at the window I'd see the frogs falling dead by the front door.

Along the front of the house were the marks where long-ago rains had washed down the rubbish from the roof. Sometimes the rain would pour down for the whole night and in the morning the house would still be wet, its colour faded.

The front steps would look clean, the rain water glistening

between the tiny cracks. Two of the steps had caved in a long time ago and a huge crack showed where the last step had become separated from the doorway.

The downstairs windows had been nailed up ever since my father's death. Sometimes I would stare into the dark rooms through the gaps in the shutters. Everything was still in its place: the wooden benches along the walls, the round table with the long legs, the old mat wrapped up in the opposite corner, while a *galabia* – perhaps one day forgotten by one of them inside – was hanging from the arm of the couch beside the reception room.

The three date palms behind the house looked washed by the rains, their branches having taken on a dark green hue.

I would wake up suddenly at night. At the time it would seem that I had been wakened by the harsh noise of rain on the roof, and I would hear my mother's soft singing. It would come and go, then I'd hear the sound of his heavy footsteps in the hallway and I'd see him as he came to a stop in front of the door of my room, his back towards me. His vast frame would shut out the light that stole into the room; his legs would be apart and he would seem to be bending forwards slightly. There would be the incessant sound of his grunting, then once again he would continue walking about.

The rain would stop, but the sound of drops falling lightly into the pools of water that had collected around the house would persist. And suddenly I'd become aware of the deep silence of the hallway and I'd imagine him standing there, by the front window, panting and trying to look out.

When I had closed the door I would still hear his snorting in the hallway, and it would have come on to rain once again.

Later, when I thought about it, it seemed to me that everything that happened started when I began locking the door of my room. Sometimes though it seems to me that that didn't effect anything at all.

I would hear his footsteps coming to a stop in front of the locked door, then the sound of his grunting through the keyhole as though he were bending his head down over it.

When the door was open he'd dash inside, panting. He would stand in the middle of the room looking around him and fumbling with the table and the things on it, then, turning round, would make off.

Sometimes he would stand in front of the closed door and push it slightly with his hand. On one occasion it opened wide and he stood there for a moment quietly, then walked around the room a little, staring about him, and went out.

Days would pass when he wouldn't go near the door and it would seem as if he'd forgotten about it. Then I'd be taken by surprise by his pushing open the door and entering. Each time he'd not turn towards me but take down the overcoat hanging on the wall and squeeze his body into it and walk about the room, his hands in the pockets. He'd stop by the table and play with the things on it. In the end the overcoat got torn under the arms.

'Son, hide it from him,' my mother would say.

But he'd wander all round the room searching for it, scattering the *galabias* that were hanging up and lifting the bedclothes and looking under the bed. When he came across it, he'd pile the things on the table and put on the overcoat and walk around the room.

I'd wake to the sound of his breathing close by me. Then, suddenly, I'd hear his grunting and he'd plunge his hand under the cover and take hold of mine and pull me from the bed. When I'd try to take away my hand, he'd strengthen his grip and I'd feel my hand being crushed in his huge palm and I'd go off behind him.

On reaching the hallway my mother would rush out. He would turn to look at me and I'd be doubled over with the pain. He'd grunt a little and let go of my hand.

With his mother he'd move round and round the table that stood in the middle of the hall, grasping the end of her *galabia*. She would leap about in front of him waving her hand. He would look at me and point to his own *galabia*. Then he'd pull me and put the end of the *galabia* in my hand, and my mother would turn towards me and her headscarf would have slipped off, and she'd gaze at me with a trembling look.

'Darling, your brother . . . your brother's playing.'

On one occasion he pulled me out of bed. He was snorting and his face looked sullen. My mother darted towards us and began to sing. He didn't turn to her but made towards the steps. Taking up the lamp, my mother followed us. Then she came to a stop by the front door; she was whispering some words I couldn't hear.

We crossed over the bridge to the other bank. When we reached the path leading to the hill he let go of my hand.

For a long time I had stopped going out with him. I saw that he still remembered the track. It had changed a lot: the trees along the two sides had been taken out and it had become bare and with many twists and turns. At the bend there were two roads branching off it. He stopped and looked at them for some time, then turned on to the road that led to the hill.

The hill looked smaller than previously. He climbed up and squatted down quietly.

The light was dim as I looked up at him. He had put his arms round his knees, with his head tilted slightly upwards. He had closed his slack mouth as he looked, sedately and quietly, at the dirt road and the carts swiftly passing along it.

I threw myself down at the bottom of the hill. I was thinking: 'If someone were to see him now, he wouldn't think anything was wrong.'

I was aware of him beginning to crawl swiftly towards me. I wanted to get away and was about to rise to my feet when he leapt on to my back and my face crashed against the ground and I felt dirt filling my nose and mouth. I violently shook my body but he seized hold of my head and pressed down with his knee on my shoulders. I lay supine for a moment and he shifted his legs and stretched them over my shoulders. Then he began pulling me up and I attempted to rise to my feet. I told myself that once I was standing up it would be easy to free myself from him. Bending my knee, I supported myself on my hands. He kept his feet on the ground, thus lightening the pressure on my shoulders until I was able to straighten myself slightly when he raised them. He was grunting and swinging his legs against my chest. Suddenly I bent

20

my whole body so as to throw him off backwards, but he fiercely clutched my face in his hands, plunging his fingers into my cheeks. Then he pulled at the corner of my mouth, turning my face in the direction he wanted to go.

I circled the hill once again. I was bowed over and it was with difficulty that I moved my feet. I was surprised I didn't fall down on the second time round.

We passed by the mulberry trees and he moved from one branch to another.

Despite myself, I felt my back arching over. With his bare thighs he pressed down on my neck; they gave off a smell of stale sweat mingled with that of earth.

Everything began swaying before my eyes. Then I was no longer able to see anything. I felt I must have stumbled many times, that I had certainly fallen. When I came to I found myself on the road while he, lying on the canal bank, was striking the water with his feet. The spray sprinkled, glittering. Then he began twisting and turning and plunging his face in among the grasses and mouthing sounds. Suddenly he grew silent and raised his head to listen. I became aware of the croaking of frogs spreading around us. I saw him get to his feet and walk for a while. Then, stretching wide his legs so as to lean down into the canal, he felt about on the surface of the water.

After that he lay down on his back, breathing heavily but without moving.

I was still squatting on my knees on the path. His breathing was regular and I guessed that maybe he had grown sleepy. Crawling towards the canal, I wet my burning face with water. As I was drying it with the end of my *galabia* I saw him resting his elbow on the ground and looking at me. He grunted slightly as he shook his foot. Then he got up and turned towards the village.

He was walking slowly, his *galabia* raised above his bandy legs. From time to time he'd turn towards me. As I tried to get to my feet I felt the pain tearing at my back, and I stumbled after him.

MOHAMMED AHMED ABDUL WALI

At a Woman's House

In front of me are left but a few small leaves of *qat*, and after a
while I'll have finished them. This accursed woman has locked
the door on me and gone off, leaving me her pale-faced son
rolled up in filthy rags. He's looking at me with surprise, perhaps
with fear. I've been shouting at him. Am I, at my time of life, to
become a nurse for a child I don't know? She's a strange one, this
woman. How can she leave her son with a strange man she's seen
for the first time? I suppose it does happen. It's not surprising in
our world.

I kept staring at the black walls of the room as darkness began
to descend over Taizz. How beautiful you are, Taizz! Every day
at this hour I would leave the place where I have my afternoon
rest and would go outside the city to where the graveyards extend
endlessly beyond its gates, and the airport road stretches out like
some legendary snake. But today I am the prisoner of a damp
room with black walls, and with dust falling down upon my head
whenever some insect passes between the ceiling boards,
perhaps a snake. How I hate snakes!

Why are you screaming, my poor child? The milk that your
mother left you hours ago is finished. Won't you leave me to my
sorrows?

I silently expelled the smoke of my cigarette and chewed the
remains of the *qat* leaves. Listen, my child: we are in one room,
neither of us knowing the other. I don't even know your name, or
how old you are. Maybe you're in your seventh month, would
that be so?

What a beautiful smile you have and how yellow your small
face is. Are you ill? My father wanted me to become a doctor one
day. They say that doctors get rich quickly in our country.

Naturally, the sick are many and you can count the number of doctors on the fingers of one hand. Don't you see, my little one, what blind chance it is that has brought us together? How beautiful your black eyes are. Be joyful and you'll kill sickness with your smile. My little one, I shall relate to you why it is that I am here. Excuse me, but I shall smoke my cigarette right down to the end. The *qat* leaves are almost finished, and I am looking at the small window high up near the ceiling where, in the black sky, swims the sad moon of Taizz near the peak of Sabir. It is, my little one, a large lamp that you will see when you grow up, suspended upon Sabir – but perhaps you will not grow up. Perhaps you will not see Sabir. I wish all our children were as robust as Sabir. Isn't that so, my little pale-faced one? I cannot tell you why I am here. Why should I bother you when you have your own sorrows and pains? You are small and when you grow up you will curse me deep inside you; you will say: What a worthless man passed by that day in my life.

Listen: I have come here to commit a small crime. Do you know Saadiyya, the brown girl, dark as coffee beans? She lives near you, in the next-door house. Yes, she always comes to your mother. I had a date with her, for us to meet today, here beside you, and when I came in some hours ago I didn't pay you any attention. You were nothing more than some tattered rags and a thin yellow body, and two tortured eyes.

She didn't come. She passed my door quickly, excusing herself to me with her eyes. Why? Because this despicable Akafi, who lives next door to you, had decided that today he would lie back and chew his *qat* near the door of his house. She can't enter for he would see her and would make a fuss which we can well do without. Little one, when he settles down in the place for his afternoon rest in front of the door of the house, he looks at Saadiyya and there's accusation in his eyes. His wife was sleeping with another man; she turned him out of the house and she spread a rug for him outside the door, where she put down his *narghile* and his *qat*, and in she went.

Don't you hear her voice in the nearby room, hissing like a snake in the arms of another man? How do I know? Don't accuse me of lying, little one: I cannot endure the way you look at me. We came in together, little one, and he sat here alongside me for a while, then went to the adjoining room where Akafi's wife, whose youthful eyes pierce the very walls of the sky with their magic, was waiting for him.

I am always unfortunate in these matters. Akafi is still gazing at the door of our room. Your mother locked the door and went off in order to give him the impression there was no one here. No, there isn't anyone apart from ourselves, and the hissing sound from his young wife.

The sad moon embraces the peak of Sabir. The stars twinkle like blue lamps. Taizz, as usual, confronts her sad night, and al-Aqaba is lit up with electric lights that are like a necklace of pearls on the breast of a beautiful woman. Saadiyya has gone to the *souk* and may not return till evening. Perhaps she's with another man. Who knows?

You see how worthless I am? Why do your eyes ask me all these questions? I cannot answer them all at one go; besides, I've finished all the *qat* leaves. If only your mother would come, I'd have her buy me some more.

The room is dark. It has made me light a match to look for the oil lamp. How unpleasant is the atmosphere of this room! The black walls and the ceiling festooned with spiders' webs, with pieces of firewood and a small stove in the corner. It seems your mother is a baker and sells bread to people in the *souk*.

Yes, I remember her sitting in front of Musa Gate by the old wall alongside the Customs. I've seen her many times, but I never thought about her. She's a young and beautiful woman. What an idiot I am. But where's your father? Don't you know? I don't either. It's ridiculous having to stay here shut up till morning. I left the shop locked up. I know that no one will come along to buy anything. Life as a whole is worthless, so what about the business of buying and selling? You see thousands of eyes staring at you as they pass by futilely in the street; they stare and go on, in search of something.

Forgive me, little one. Have you never once seen Taizz? You have seen it, though: your mother has carried you through its streets. Don't you agree with me that Taizz is the most beautiful city in the world – the mountain of Sabir when it is wrapped around with its cloak of clouds in the afternoon, as it gazes at Taizz with the tenderness of a giant father? Taizz is wonderful.

Yes, I was born in it and so were you. It is our city. When you grow up I shall have grown old, but our city will be youthful. There in the midst of Sabir the most beautiful houses in the world will be built, and the Qahira Citadel is a superb place for building an international hotel. Let's dream of the future. With lights made by electric suns. Is that not better than this yellow oil lamp which resembles your small face?

Your mother hasn't come yet. I'm thinking of her. She's beautiful. I'm still hearing the hissing of the young woman, and the sound of the waterpipe as Akafi draws on it. As his wife is being unfaithful to him the other side of the wall, he stuffs his mouth with *qat* and puffs out smoke from a toothless mouth. His appearance is disgusting, just like this room. Water has spilt from the earthenware jar over there by the door, and the oven is covered with dust and firewood and inside it frightening reptiles crawl about, while your mother's clothes are hanging straight above my head. I smell the odour of woman. How stupid I am! Why don't I leave this hell?

The sound of the door being opened. She has come. I shall talk to her and tell her to stay with me. Her white face, as she steps through the door, excites me, also the hissing noises of the young woman and the sounds of my friend's kisses. Listen, my dear, haven't you locked the door so we can be here together? Why? Don't you know? I don't want Saadiyya, let her go to hell. I need a woman. Do you understand? Where are you going to? There's no one there, the world's grown dark, the moon has disappeared, and your poor little one went to sleep hours ago. There's no one left but us – I and the animal that's screaming inside me. You're going to have a wash? Then bring me a little *qat* and come back quickly.

The devil take you – she's beautiful. Why didn't I notice her before? How stupid I am! Are you still sleeping, my orphan child? That's better for you than to see a wild animal alongside you.

A curse on this silence and this putrid smell. The lamp grows faint and sends out its light as pale as life in the streets of Taizz. The sound of the waterpipe has ceased. Perhaps he has returned to his room. Has your beautiful wife returned? How watchful you are! She's beautiful, your wife. I congratulate you on her.

She has the same beauty as our country.

The door is again opened. Let me move your child from this place. I can't stay beside him. Take him. Yes, give him to your neighbour and lock the door.

Why are you turning off the lamp? How warm you are, how warm!

I'm stupid. Where were you all this time?

Why hadn't I noticed her before? Why was I running after Saadiyya?

The night falls over Taizz, and the sad moon has its face covered by clouds, and Sabir is wrapped in mist, while the animal inside of me dies . . . dies . . . dies.

MOHAMMED KHUDAYYIR

Clocks Like Horses

This meeting may take place. I shall get my watch repaired and go out to the quays of the harbour, then at the end of the night I shall return to the hotel and find him sleeping in my bed, his face turned to the wall, having hung his red turban on the clothes hook.

Till today I still own a collection of old watches; I had come by them from an uncle of mine who used to be a sailor on the ships of the Andrew Weir company; old pocket watches with chains and silver-plated cases, all contained in a small wooden box in purses of shiny blue cloth. While my interest in them has of late waned, I had, as a schoolboy, been fascinated by them. I would take them out from their blue purses and scrutinize their workings in an attempt to discover something about them that would transcend 'time stuffed like old cotton in a small cushion', as I had recorded one day in my diary.

One day during the spring school holidays I was minded to remove one of these watches from its box and to put it into the pocket of my black suit, attaching its chain to the buttonholes of my waistcoat. For a long time I wandered round the chicken market before seating myself at a café. The waiter came and asked me the time. I calmly took the watch out of its blue purse. My watch was incapable of telling the time, like the other watches in the box, nothing in it working except for the spring of the case which was no sooner pressed than it flicked open revealing a pure white dial and two hands that stood pointing to two of the Roman numerals on the face. Before I could inform him that the watch was not working, the waiter had bent down and pulled the short chain towards him; having looked attentively at the watch he closed its case on which had been engraved a sailing ship within a frame of foreign writing. Then, giving it back to me, he stood up straight.

'How did you get hold of it?'

'I inherited it from a relative of mine.'

I returned the watch to its place.

'Was your relative a sailor?'

'Yes.'

'Only three or four of the famous sailors are still alive.'

'My relative was called Mughamis.'

'Mughamis? I don't know him.'

'He wouldn't settle in one place. He died in Bahrain.'

'That's sailors for you! Do you remember another sailor called Marzouk? Since putting ashore for the last time he has been living in Fao. He opened a shop there for repairing watches, having learned the craft from the Portuguese. He alone would be able to repair an old watch like yours.'

I drank down the glass of tea and said to the waiter as I paid him: 'Did you say he was living in Fao?'

'Yes, near the hotel.'

The road to Fao is a muddy one and I went on putting off the journey until one sunny morning I took my place among the passengers in a bus which set off loaded with luggage. The passengers, who sat opposite one another in the middle of the bus, exchanged no words except for general remarks about journeying in winter, about how warm this winter was, and other comments about the holes in the road. At the moment they stopped talking I took out my watch. Their eyes became fixed on it, but no one asked me about it or asked the time. Then we began to avoid looking at each other and transferred our attentions to the vast open countryside and to the distant screen of date palms in the direction of the east that kept our vehicle company and hid the villages along the Shatt al-Arab.

We arrived at noon and someone showed me to the hotel which lies at the intersection of straight roads and looks on to a square in the middle of which is a round fenced garden. The hotel consisted of two low storeys, while the balcony that overlooked the square was at such a low height that someone in the street could have climbed up on to it. I, who cannot bear the smell of hotels, or the heavy, humid shade in their hallways in daytime, hastened to call out to its owners. When I repeated my call, a boy looked down from a door at the side and said: 'Do you want to sleep here?'

'Have you a place?' I said.

The boy went into the room and from it there emerged a man whom I asked for a room with a balcony. The boy who was showing me the way informed me that the hotel would be empty by day and packed at night. Just as the stairway was the shortest of stairways and the balcony the lowest of balconies, my room was the smallest and contained a solitary bed, but the sun entered it from the balcony. I threw my bag on to the bed and the boy sat down beside me. 'The doors are all without locks,' said the boy. 'Why should we lock them – the travellers only stay for one night.'

Then he leaned towards me and whispered: 'Are you Indian?'

This idea came as a surprise to me. The boy himself was more likely to be Indian with his dark complexion, thick brilliantined hair and sparkling eyes. I whispered to him: 'Did they tell you that Basra used to be called the crotch of India, and that the Indian invaders in the British army, who came down to the land of Fao first of all, desired no other women except those of Basra?'

The boy ignored my cryptic reference to the mixing of passions and blending of races and asked, if I wasn't Indian, where did I live?

'I've come from Ashar,' I told him, 'on a visit to the watch-maker. Would you direct me to him?'

'Perhaps you mean the old man who has many clocks in his house,' said the boy.

'Yes, that must be he,' I said.

'He's not far from the hotel,' he said. 'He lives alone with his daughter and never leaves the house.'

The boy brought us lunch from a restaurant, and we sat on the bed to eat, and he told me about the man I had seen downstairs: 'He's not the owner of the hotel, just a permanent guest.'

Then, with his mouth full of food, he whispered: 'He's got a pistol.'

'You know a lot of things, O Indian,' I said, also speaking in a whisper.

29

He protested that he wasn't Indian but was from Hasa. He had a father who worked on the ships that transported dates from Basra to the coastal towns of the Gulf and India.

The boy took me to the watchmaker, leaving me in front of the door of his house. A gap made by a slab of stone that had been removed from its place in the upper frieze of the door made this entrance unforgettable. One day, in tropical years, there had stopped near where I was a sailor shaky with sickness, or some Sikh soldier shackled with lust, and he had looked at the slab of stone on which was engraved some date or phrase, before continuing on his unknown journey. And after those two there perhaps came some foreign archaeologist whose boat had been obstructed by the silt and who had put up in the town till the water rose, and his curiosity for things Eastern had been drawn to the curves of the writing on the slab of stone and he had torn it out and carried it off with him to his boat. Now I, likewise, was in front of this gateway to the sea.

On the boy's advice I did not hesitate to push open the door and enter into what looked like a porch which the sun penetrated through apertures near the ceiling and in which I was confronted by hidden and persistent ticking sounds and a garrulous ringing that issued from the pendulums and hammers of large clocks of the type that strike the hours, ranged along the two sides of the porch. As I proceeded one or more clocks struck at the same time. All the clocks were similar in size, in the great age of the wood of their frames, and in the shape of their round dials, their Roman numerals, and their delicate arrow-like hands – except that these hands were pointing to different times.

I had to follow the slight curve of the porch to come unexpectedly upon the last of the great sailors in his den, sitting behind a large table on which was heaped the wreckage of clocks. He was occupied with taking to pieces the movement of a clock by the light of a shaded lamp that hung down from the ceiling at a height close to his frail, white-haired head. He looked towards me with a glance from one eye that was naked and another on which a magnifying-glass had been fixed, then went back to disassembling the movement piece by piece. The short glance was sufficient to link this iron face with the nuts, cogwheels and hands of the movements of the many clocks hanging on the walls and thrown into corners under dust and rust. Clocks that didn't work and others that did, the biggest of them being a clock on the wall above the watchmaker's head, which was, to be precise, the movement of a large grandfather clock made of brass, the dial of which had been removed and which had been divested of its cabinet so that time manifested itself in it naked and shining, sweeping along on its serrated cogwheels in a regular mechanical sequence: from the rotation of the spring to the pendulum that swung harmoniously to and fro and ended in the slow, tremulous, imperceptible movement of the hands. When the cogwheels had taken the hands along a set distance of time's journey, the striking cogwheel would move and raise the hammer. I had not previously seen a naked, throbbing clock and thus I became mesmerized by the regular throbbing that synchronized with the swinging motion of the pendulum and with the movement of the cogwheels of various diameters. I started at the sound of the hammer falling against the bell; the gallery rang with three strokes whose reverberations took a long time to die away, while the other clocks went on, behind the glass of their cabinets, with their incessant ticking.

The watchmaker raised his head and asked me if the large clock above his head had struck three times.

Then, immersing himself in taking the mechanism to pieces, he said: 'Like horses; like horses running on the ocean bed.'

A clock in the porch struck six times and he said: 'Did one of them strike six times? It's six in America. They're getting up now, while the sun is setting in Burma.'

Then the room was filled again with noisy reverberations. 'Did it strike seven? It's night-time in Indonesia. Did you make out the last twelve strokes? They are fast asleep in the furthest west of the world. After some hours the sun will rise in the furthest east. What time is it? Three? That's our time, here near the Gulf.'

One clock began striking on its own. After a while the chimes blended with the tolling of other clocks as hammers coincided in falling upon bells, and others landed halfway between the times of striking and yet others fell between these halfways so that the chimes hurried in pursuit of one another in a confused scale. Then, one after another, the hammers became still, the chimes growing further apart, till a solitary clock remained, the last clock that had not discharged all its time, letting it trickle out now in a separate, high-pitched reverberation.

He was holding my watch in his grasp. 'Several clocks might strike together,' he said, 'strike as the fancy takes them. I haven't liked to set my clocks to the same time. I have assigned to my daughter the task of merely winding them up. They compete with one another like horses. I have clocks that I bought from people who looted them from the houses of Turkish employees who left them as they hurried away after the fall of Basra. I also got hold of clocks that were left behind later on by the Jews who emigrated. Friends of mine, the skippers of ships, who would come to visit me here, would sell me clocks of European manufacture. Do you see the clock over there in the passageway? It was in the house of the Turkish commander of the garrison of Fao's fortress.'

I saw the gleam of the quick-swinging pendulum behind glass in the darkness of the cabinets of the clocks in the porch. Then I asked him about my watch. 'Your watch? It's a rare one. They're no longer made. I haven't handled such a watch for a long time. I'm not sure about it but I'll take it to pieces. Take a stroll round and come back here at night.'

That was what I'd actually intended to do. I would return before night. The clocks bade me farewell with successive chimes. Four chimes in Fao: seven p.m. in the swarming streets of Calcutta. Four chimes: eight a.m. in the jungles of Buenos Aires . . . Outside the den the clamour had ceased, also the smell of engine oil and of old wood.

I returned at sunset. I had spent the time visiting the old barracks which had been the home of the British army of occupation, then I had sat in a café near the fish market.

I didn't find the watchmaker in his former place, but presently I noticed a huge empty cabinet that had been moved into a gap between the clocks. The watchmaker was in an open courtyard before an instrument made up of clay vessels, which I guessed to be a type of water-clock. When he saw me he called out: 'Come here. Come, I'll show you something.'

I approached the vessels hanging on a cross-beam: from them water dripped into a vessel hanging on another, lower cross-beam; the water then flowed on to a metal plate on the ground, in which there was a gauge for measuring the height of the water.

'A water-clock?'

'Have you seen one like it?'

'I've read about them. They were the invention of people of old.'

'The Persians call them *bingan*.'

'I don't believe it tells the right time.'

'No, it doesn't, it reckons only twenty hours to the day. According to its reckoning I'm 108 years old instead of ninety, and it is seventy-eight years since the British entered Basra instead of sixty. I learned how to make it from a Muscati sailor who had one like it in his house on the coast.'

I followed him to the den, turning to two closed doors in the small courtyard on which darkness had descended. He returned the empty clock-cabinet to its place and seated himself in his chair. His many clothes lessened his appearance of senility; he was lost under his garments, one over another and yet another over them, his head inside a vast tarbush.

'I've heard you spent a lifetime at sea.'

'Yes. It's not surprising that our lives are always linked to water. I was on one of the British India ships as a syce with an English trader dealing in horses.'

He toyed with the remnants of the watches in front of him, then said: 'He used to call himself by an Arabic name. We would call him Surour Saheb. He used to buy Nejdi horses from the rural areas of the south and they would then be shipped to Bombay where they would be collected up and sent to the racecourses in England. Fifteen days on end at sea, except that we would make stops at the Gulf ports. We would stop for some days in Muscat. When there were strong winds against us we would spend a month at sea. The captains, the cooks and the pilots were Indians, while the others, seamen and syces, were from Muscat, Hasa and Bahrain; the rest were from the islands of the Indian Ocean. We would have with us divers from Kuwait. I remember their small dark bodies and plaited hair as they washed down the horses on the shore or led them to the ship. I was the youngest syce. I began my first sea journey at the age of twelve. I joined the ship with my father who was an assistant to the captain and responsible for looking after the stores and equipment. There were three of us, counting my father, who would sleep in the storeroom among the sacks and barrels of tar, the fish oil, ropes and dried fish, on beds made up of coconut fibre.'

'Did you make a lot?'

'We? We didn't make much. The trader did. Each horse would fetch 800 rupees in Bombay, and when we had reached Bengal it would fetch 1,500 rupees. On our return to Basra we would receive our wages for having looked after the horses. Some of us would buy goods from India and sell them on our return journey wherever we put in: cloth, spices, rice, sugar, perfumes, and wood, and sometimes peacocks and monkeys.'

'Did you employ horses in the war?'

'I myself didn't take part in the war. Of course they used them. When the Turks prevented us from trading with them because they needed them for the army, we moved to the other side of the river. We had a corral and a caravanserai for sleeping in at Khorramshahr. From there we began to smuggle out the horses far from the clutches of the Turkish customs men. On the night when we'd be travelling we'd feed and water the horses well and at dawn we'd proceed to the corral and each syce would lead out his horse. As for me I was required to look after the transportation of the provisions and fodder; other boys who were slightly older than me were put in charge of the transportation of the water, the ropes, the chains and other equipment. The corral was close to the shore, except that the horses would make a lot of noise and stir up dust when they were being pulled along by the reins to the ship that would lie at the end of an anchorage stretching out to it from the shore. The ship would rock and tiny bits of straw would become stuck on top of our heads while the syces would call the horses by their names, telling them to keep quiet, until they finished tying them up in their places. It was no easy matter, for during the journey the waves, or the calm of the invisible sea, would excite one of the horses or would make it ill, so that its syce would have to spend the night with it, watching over it and keeping it company. As we lay in our sleeping quarters we would hear the syce reassuring his horse with some such phrase as: 'Calm down. Calm down, my Precious Love. The grass over there is better.' However this horse, whose name was Precious Love, died somewhere near Aden. At dawn the sailors took it up and consigned it to the waves. It was a misty morning and I was carrying a lantern, and I heard the great carcase hitting the water, though without seeing it; I did, though, see its syce's face close to me – he would be returning from his voyage without any earnings.'

Two or three clocks happened to chime together. I said to him:

'Used you to put in to Muscat?'

'Yes. Did I tell you about our host in Muscat? His wooden house was on the shore of a small bay, opposite an old stone fortress on the other side. We would set out for his house by boat. By birth he was a highlander, coming from the tribes in the mountains facing the bay. He was also a sorcerer. He was a close friend of Surour Saheb, supplying him with a type of ointment the Muscati used to prepare out of mountain herbs, which the Englishman would no sooner smear on his face than it turned a dark green and would gleam in the lamplight like a wave among rocks. In exchange for this the Muscati would get tobacco from him. I didn't join them in smoking, but I was fond of chewing a type of olibanum that was to be found extensively in the markets of the coast. I would climb up into a high place in the room that had been made as a permanent bed and would watch them puffing out the smoke from the *narghiles* into the air as they lay relaxing round the fire, having removed their dagger-belts and placed them in front of them alongside their coloured turbans. Their beards would be plunged in the smoke and the rings would glitter in their ears under the combed locks of hair whenever they turned towards the merchant, lost in thought. The merchant, relaxing on feather cushions, would be wearing brightly-coloured trousers of Indian cloth and would be wrapped round in an *aba* of Kashmir wool; as for his silk turban, he would, like the sailors, have placed it in front of him beside his pistol.'

'Did you say that the Muscati was a sorcerer?'

'He had a basket of snakes in which he would lay one of the

sailors, then bring him out alive. His sparse body would be swallowed in his lustrous flowing robes, as was his small head in his saffron-coloured turban with the tassels. We were appalled at his repulsive greed for food, for he would eat a whole basketful of dates during a night and would drink enough water to provide for ten horses. He was amazing, quite remarkable; he would perform bizarre acts; swallowing a puff from his *narghile*, he would after a while begin to release the smoke from his mouth and nose for five consecutive minutes. You should have seen his stony face, with the clouds of smoke floating against it like serpents that flew and danced. He was married to seven women for whom he had dug out, in the foot of the mountain, rooms that overlooked the bay. No modesty prevented him from disclosing their fabulous names: Mountain Flower, Daylight Sun, Sea Pearl, Morning Star. He was a storehouse of spicy stories and tales of strange travels and we would draw inspiration from him for names for our horses. At the end of the night he would leave us sleeping and would climb up the mountain. At the end of one of our trips we stayed as his guest for seven nights, during which time men from the Muscati's tribe visited us to have a smoke; they would talk very little and would look with distaste at the merchant and would then leave quietly with their antiquated rifles.

'Our supper would consist of spiced rice and grilled meat or fish. We would be given a sweet sherbet to drink in brass cups. As for the almond-filled *halva* of Muscat that melts in the mouth, even the bitter coffee could not disperse its scented taste. In the morning he would return and give us some sherbet to drink that would settle our stomachs, which would be suffering from the night's food and drink, and would disperse the tobacco fumes from the sailors' heads.'

An outburst of striking clocks prevented him momentarily from enlarging further. He did not wait for the sound to stop before continuing:

'On the final night of our journey he overdid his tricks in quite a frightening manner. While the syces would seek help from his magic in treating their sick horses, they were afraid nonetheless that the evil effects of his magic would spread and reap the lives of these horses. And thus it was that a violent wind drove our ship on to a rock at the entrance to the bay and smashed it. Some of us escaped drowning, but the sorcerer of Muscat was not among them. He was travelling with the ship on his way to get married to a woman from Bombay; but the high waves choked his shrieks and eliminated his magic.'

'And the horses?'

'They combated the waves desperately. They were swimming in the direction of the rocky shore, horses battling against the white horses of the waves. All of them were drowned. That was my last journey in the horse ships. After that, in the few years that preceded the war, I worked on the mail ships.'

He made a great effort to remember and express himself:

'In Bahrain I married a woman who bore me three daughters whom I gave in marriage to sons of the sea. I stayed on there with the boatbuilders until after the war. Then, in the thirties, I returned to Basra and bought the clocks and settled in Fao, marrying a woman from here.'

'You are one of the few sailors who are still alive today.'

He asked me where I lived and I told him that I had put up at the hotel. He said:

'A friend of mine used to live in it. I don't know if he's still alive – for twenty years I haven't left my house.'

Then, searching among the fragments of watches, he asked me in surprise:

'Did you come to Fao just because of the watch?'

I answered him that there were some towns one had to go to. He handed me my watch. It was working. Before placing it in my hand he scrutinized its flap on which had been engraved a ship with a triangular sail, which he said was of the type known as *sunbuk*.

I opened the flap. The hands were making their slow way round. The palms of my hand closed over the watch, and we listened to the sea echoing in the clocks of the den. The slender legs of horses run in the streets of the clock faces, are abducted in the glass of the large grandfather clocks. The clocks tick and strike: resounding hooves, chimes driven forward like waves. A chime: the friction of chains and ropes against wet wood. Two chimes: the dropping of the anchor into the blue abyss. Three: the call of the rocks. Four: the storm blowing up. Five: the neighing of the horses. Six . . . seven . . . eight . . . nine . . . ten . . . eleven . . . twelve . . .

This winding lane is not large enough to allow a lorry to pass, but it lets in a heavy damp night and sailors leading their horses, and a man dizzy from sea-sickness, still holding in his grasp a pocket watch and making an effort to avoid the water and the gentle sloping of the lane and the way the walls curve round. The bends increase with the thickening darkness and the silence. Light seeps through from the coming bend, causing me to quicken my step. In its seeping through and the might of its radiation it seems to be marching against the wall, carving into the damp brickwork folds of skins and crumpled faces that are the masks of seamen and traders from different races who have passed by here before me and are to be distinguished only by their headgear: the bedouin of Nejd and the rural areas of the south by the *kuffiyeh* and *'iqal*, the Iraqi effendis of the towns by the *sidara*; the Persians by the black tarbooshes made of goat-skin; the Ottoman officers, soldiers and government employees by their tasselled tarbooshes; the Indians by their red turbans; the Jews by flat red tarbooshes; the monks and missionaries by their black head coverings; the European sea captains by their naval caps; the explorers in disguise . . . They rushed out towards the rustling noise coming from behind the last bend, the eerie rumbling, the bated restlessness of the waves below the high balustrades . . . Then, here are Fao's quays, the lamps leading its wooden bridges along the water for a distance; in the spaces between them boats are anchored one alongside another, their lights swaying; there is also a freighter with its lights on, anchored between the two middle berths. It was possible for me to make out in the middle of the river scattered floating lights. I didn't go very close to the quay installations but contented myself with standing in front of the dark, bare extension of the river. To my surprise a man who was perhaps working as a watchman or worker on the quays approached me and asked me for the time. Eleven.

On my return to the hotel I took a different road, passing by the closed shops. I was extremely alert. The light will be shining brightly in the hotel vestibule. The oil stove will be in the middle of it, and to one side of the vestibule will be baggage, suitcases, a watercooling box and a cupboard. Seated on the bench will be a man who is dozing, his cigarette forgotten between his fingers. It will happen that I shall approach the door of my room, shall open the door, and shall find him sleeping in my bed; he will be turned to the wall, having hung his red turban on the clothes hook.

BAHAA TAHER

Advice from a Sensible Young Man

The old man ran after him as he was crossing Talaat Harb Street, just by the Radio Cinema. He called out loudly to him: 'Mr Adil!' He heard the screech of tyres as a driver strove to bring his car to a sudden stop, then began cursing the old man, who paid no attention, catching up with his friend before he'd reached the pavement and grasping his arm with thin, clutching fingers. For a while they looked at each other without talking, then Adil pushed away the hand from his arm and asked him what he wanted.

The old man said: 'It's me, Mr Adil. Me. Don't you remember me? Every day you used to buy *al-Ahram* from me and *al-Kawakeb* every week. I used to stand at the corner of your street. I'm Khalil, your "Uncle" Khalil.'

'Yes,' said Adil. 'And you, don't *you* remember? We've met here often. We met a week ago and I gave you some advice. Don't you remember?'

He began walking slowly, with Uncle Khalil following: just a pace behind him all the time so that he could touch his arm as he spoke. 'Ah, Your Excellency, I do remember. But you don't know – thanks be to God, I've changed. Please listen to me. I've changed absolutely. By Almighty God, by Almighty God, I no longer have anything to do with opium. I don't know what it looks like or what it tastes like. May it burn in hell!'

Adil again came to a stop and the thin old man with the glazed eyes faced him. His eyes discharged small tears that he didn't notice and he was continually passing his tongue over his lips.

'You told me that last time,' said Adil. 'You said you'd given it up and wanted to work. Why aren't you working?' Uncle Khalil lowered his head; with its thinning white hair it looked tiny between the grey jacket's wide shoulders that shone with the blackness of dirt. Then he raised his head and said: 'How's the Hagg's health? And your esteemed father?'

Adil gave a short laugh and said: 'Fine.'

Then he walked off again with Uncle Khalil following him and saying: 'Real gentlemen they are.'

After a long silence he said in a weak voice: 'To tell you the truth, Excellency, I'm now under treatment. The fact is the drug ruined my chest, God burn it in hell and the day I got to know it. The fact is Your Excellency doesn't know. Remember your Uncle Khalil in days gone by? By God, Bey, I knew only my work and my home. I'd begrudge myself a cup of coffee, telling myself the piastre would be better spent on the home. It all started because some people made a fool of me. They told me opium cures rheumatism, and I got hooked and it ruined me. There's also the worry of the house and the kids. Five children and their mother, and money's the devil to come by. It's a heavy burden on your Uncle Khalil. It's really awful, Excellency, when a fellow's worries get the better of him. Thanks be to God, though, the good Lord came to my rescue and I'll be going back to work after I've had treatment for my chest. Please be so good as to help me and I'll pay you back when . . . when . . .'

Suddenly he stopped, then began coughing violently, his hand to his mouth. Adil slowed down, turning his head slightly towards the old man who was standing there, wracked with coughing, almost out of sight in the crowd. The man hurried to catch up with him before he had gone too far and said in a gasping voice broken by short coughs:

'No, no, I can't work before I've had treatment for my chest. Just some help, a little help, if you'd be so kind, and I'll pay you back.'

Quietly, without turning to him, Adil said: 'You're lying, Uncle Khalil. You don't want to have treatment for your chest or anything of the sort. All you want is to buy that rubbish. How many times have I given you good advice? The last time I gave you ten piastres, didn't I? What did you do with them? You spent them on the drug, didn't you?'

'Ten piastres?' said Uncle Khalil in protest. 'By God, Bey, with ten piastres you don't buy . . . As I told you, Bey, the drug's

41

a thing of the past – honestly. Now it's out of the question – if Your Excellency would like to come along with me . . .'

The young man came to a stop in the street and said in a firm, impatient tone: 'Look here, I've got just one thing to say to you: you've got to get yourself treated. Go into a clinic so they can treat you. If you want somebody with some influence, I've got a doctor friend who'd be able . . .' The old man stretched out his hand and once again grasped Adil's arm.

'Let's go,' he said quickly. 'At once. I'll come right along with you. May God prosper you. Let's go right away to your doctor friend.'

Adil began looking in confusion at the old trembling man who was grasping his arm as he tried to think of something to say to him. Before he spoke, however, Uncle Khalil broke in with: 'But, Bey, before going to the doctor, if I could just see my children first. I must see my children, make arrangements for them. They're poor things, Bey. How would they be fed if I were to go into the clinic? I'm just asking. Excuse me for saying such a thing, but do you want their mother to go around selling herself? Would you be happy at such a thing, Bey? Would you be happy? I . . . actually I didn't tell you. The fact is I did go into a clinic. You see, I treated myself and got cured, thanks be to God.

'It's now a question of my chest and cough. I want to go to the doctor for him to have a look at my chest, by which I mean have an X-ray. Please help me, Bey. Just the doctor's fee.'

They were standing in front of the Miami Cinema at a crowded point of the street, with people pushing at them in order to get through the crush. Adil found himself right in front of the stills advertising the film being shown and discovered that for some-time he had been staring at the picture of the beautiful heroine reclining on a bed, her hair in disarray and her dress drawn up over her raised thighs, and that he had hardly heard anything of what Uncle Khalil had been saying. Bringing him to mind, he shook his arm free and said:

'I've said what I have to say. That's it.'

When he walked on again, the old man gave a few short laughs and nodded his head like someone who's discovered some secret, and said: 'I understand, Bey. You're worried about me. You're worried about your Uncle Khalil, but, as I said, I've found work, thanks be to God. I'll open a newspaper kiosk and go back to being what I was. God willing, I'll go back to being better than I was.' Then he added in a lowered voice: 'The long and short of it is – and let's be frank – there's not a bite of food in the house. Be so good as to help me. All I want is enough for the children's food.'

'What do you care about your children?' said Adil irritably. 'All you care about is that wretched opium.'

'Even an opium addict,' said the old man, 'is a human being, Your Excellency. I too love my children.'

'It's out of the question,' said Adil. 'A man who leaves his work and his home for the sake of . . . How many times have I told you? Look at me. I'm an engineer. I work night and day, in the government and with a company. I kill myself in order to earn money. Why? Have I, for example, bought myself a car so at least to spare myself the difficulties of public transport? Not at all. Every millieme I earn I put aside to protect my son's future. It's true he's still at nursery school but a man's got to take account of the future, Uncle Khalil. Who knows what other children are on the way. A man's got to assure himself about the future and after that he can start thinking about himself. Why can't you benefit from advice, Uncle Khalil? Look at the people around you. Look at myself.'

The old man was listening to him and nodding his head in agreement at his words, though his eyes strayed about, showing that he was not following what was being said. When the engineer had finished he said to him: 'Quite right, sir. Thanks be to God. As I said to you, the good Lord has cured me.' Then he gave a sudden short laugh. 'You were just so high when you used to come and buy the newspaper for your dad. "Uncle Khalil – al-Ahram." Remember?' Then he again came to a stop and seized the engineer's hand.

'Have pity on me, Bey – I kiss your hand.'

The engineer quickly released his hand. 'We've had enough of such talk,' he said and began to walk off quickly, with the old man running close behind him and saying: 'Any sort of help, Bey. Anything.'

'Go back to your children and come to your senses.'

'I'll be sensible, Bey. I'll do everything you say – honestly.

43

Your Excellency would like me to put my children into nursery school, isn't that so? I will, I will, but I'm in need of help, I'm . . .'

Again the old man stretched out his hand and seized the engineer by the shoulder, almost forcibly bringing him to a stop. He brought his face up close: his eyes were watering all the time and the muscles of his face twitched convulsively.

'Listen,' he said in a whisper. 'There's no point in our putting on an act. You don't have to be shy with your Uncle Khalil. You're a real man and I'd like to do you a favour. Just listen and don't say anything. Between you and me, you see, I know a woman who's a real beauty. No, don't say a word. After all, you're only young once so you might as well enjoy yourself. I tell you – a real beauty. All I have to do is bring her to you. Don't say anything – your Uncle Khalil wants to do you a favour.'

'Have you gone mad, man?' said the engineer.

'Listen,' said the old man. 'I know you. You've always been a man who's known how to enjoy himself. I saw you with girls many a time and I never said a thing. Look, your Uncle Khalil never opens his mouth. No, don't say anything.'

The old man put his finger to his mouth, then wiped his eyes with the back of his hand, though his sunken cheek remained wet. He began letting out short, staccato laughs as he talked in a hurried whisper.

'I don't open my mouth because I like people who can keep a secret. I don't want a thing from you – the taxi fare and all I have to do is bring her to you. You haven't so much as said a single kind word to your Uncle Khalil, but no matter. What's it matter? You see, you're like a son to me . . . You see, I wouldn't do this, not for another human being, but if you'd like to help your Uncle Khalil – see, look here, all I want is the taxi fare. Listen, if you don't believe me, take my identity card till I get back.'

With trembling hands he began searching in the inner pocket of his jacket, while fresh tears began seeping from his eyes.

'Have you sunk so low?' said the engineer. 'You're better off dead.'

Leaving him, he walked away quickly, almost breaking into a run. The old man, who had succeeded in extracting his identity card, stood where he was, waving the card at him and saying:

'Come, Your Excellency. You haven't understood me. You haven't understood.'

When the old man saw the other once again crossing the street, he ran after him. As the brakes gave out a scream and something heavy banged into him in the street, the old man fell to the ground. His whole body, waist high, rose up and he said 'Ah' before falling back again with arms outspread and the card slipping from his grasp and coming to rest alongside him on the ground.

This was after sunset, in the last glow of light before darkness descended. The driver of the car got out in a state of alarm as he looked at the white-haired man with the open eyes, a dark circle of passers-by having collected round the white car. Someone said: 'Just a while ago I saw him talking to a man.' Another said: 'Yes, a young man, and I saw him cross the street.' But when they looked round for this young man they couldn't find him.

He too had witnessed the accident and had started off back to see what had happened. But suddenly he had stopped and said to himself: 'They'll take me as a witness and they'll keep me need-lessly and I'm already late for getting to the company' and he had hurried into the passageway he'd reached. Having gone some way, he again came to a stop and decided to return, but said to himself: 'If he's been injured they'll give him treatment and maybe he'll get compensation, and if he's dead there's nothing to be done and maybe his children will get some compensation to help them along.' Though his heart was beating quickly, he walked off hurriedly and did not return.

Someone bent over and picked up the old man's card. He examined it, reading his name and the names of his children before giving it to the policeman, who was listening in silence to the driver. The latter was explaining how the accident had occurred, pointing with both hands to his own chest, then waving them at the dead man though without looking at him.

YUSUF SHAROUNI

Glimpses from the Life of Maugoud Abdul Maugoud and Two Postscripts

The two candles went out: the girl and her mother, my wife and my mistress, and nothing remains but the slippers.

I am a teacher of philosophy, having been a student of philosophy for a long, long time – but let's start the story from its end.

I am on my own in the room; a solitary, lonely room on the spacious roof where the inhabitants hang their washing on lines strung across it haphazardly, sometimes cutting across each other, sometimes running parallel and making triangles and squares. There's not much furniture in my room: a chair on the seat of which I sit and on the back of which I hang my suit; a table for writing at and eating on; a sofa on which my guests sit during the day and on which I sleep at night; a tumbler from which I sometimes drink and in which, at other times, I place the sweet peas I'm fond of. Everything in my room is dual-purpose, even the newspaper which the vendor each day throws under the door and in which I follow the news of my indictment, and which I then employ as a tablecloth. But let's start the story from its end.

How terrified I am of the night! How gloomy is the night! It is not the night at its beginning that's my trouble but the last parts of night. I flee from my fear at the beginnings of night when a deep sleep descends upon me directly after having supper, be it ever so light, just as though I have taken some potent drug. It is not long, though, before I find that I have been the victim of an abominable piece of deception, for I wake up in alarm at three or four in the morning when the silence of night becomes louder than the din of day: the barking of a dog, the croaking of a frog, the striking of a clock, things breaking, footsteps approaching, and the anticipation of evil that is on the point of occurring, does not occur but will occur. A thought revolves round my mind, telling me: set a limit, a solution to the situation you're in; open the windows of your room when the day jostles with God's creatures, to announce your crime. In fact, it would be best for you to slip off without fuss to the police station and confess. But to what shall I confess? Shall I confess that I am not at all certain as to what to confess? But do you think they'll wait till I go by myself? Perhaps they are coming, for if not why does a dog bark, why the tread of footsteps? How terrible are sleeplessness and anxiety! The dawn is my escape from my torture: the crowing of cocks, the chirping of sparrows, and the nightmare of darkness is banished.

On a morning at some time far distant, I was going down the stairs on my way to the college when there came to my nose a putrid smell. At first I thought it was coming from some dead cat or dog, or perhaps from a rat that the children of the building had thrown into the stairwell. However, the disappearane of Sheikha Madeeha some days ago brought doubts to my mind, she who used to fill the building, the lane, the whole quarter with activity and noise. I climbed back up the stairs I had descended to knock at the door of her flat. However no one answered my knocking. In vain I tried to make out the truth through the locked door; placing my eye at it, I could see nothing; listening carefully, I could hear nothing. My nose alone was able to pick out a smell that came nearest to that of the crime. I decided to hurry off to the police station to inform them of my fears, for more than one bond had, before she had taken to religion several weeks ago, tied me to Sheikha Madeeha.

When I made it known to her that people's eyes were opened and that there was no sense in being accused of something of which we were guiltless, her answer – as though I had made a joke – was a laugh.

'Why don't you marry?'

'I'm still a student.'

'And you don't have the money to maintain a wife?'

'Nor have I made a choice of a bride.'

'The bride is before you, the money is guaranteed, the home already set up.'

Thus it was that she proposed marriage to me, though to her daughter: an answer that would silence people's gossiping, an explanation that would not occur to the Devil himself for the secret visits that were exchanged, and a final elimination of my fears. There was nothing for me to do but go down from my room on top to her flat as a husband to her daughter before people, and as a lover to her before the Devil. What a bed of sin! How unfortunate our victim! What a mad woman to snatch both me and her daughter up in her whims! I, though, happy with killing two birds, strike up my philosophical anthem: I am frightened, therefore I exist.

On my way back with the police there was some hope that my fears were sheer imagining and that we would find the door open and Sheikha Madeeha standing and barring the way to the police, for should anything bad have happened to Sheikha Madeeha I'd be caused endless trouble and I'd be the first person to be accused. When I was asked to attend before the examining magistrate I was trembling with fear. I gave a résumé of my connection with Sheikha Madeeha, denying and expressing repugnance at the thought of any sinful relationship with her; certain meddlesome witnesses had informed the examining magistrate of possibilities of this nature. I admitted that on Thursday morning I had paid her a debt I owed her.

'What debt?'

'A loan I made of her the day of my marriage to her daughter.'

'How much did you give her?'

'Two pounds as a first instalment.'

As for my battle with her, I did not refer to it at all. A piece of her daughter's shoe, with its faded red colour, was lying in front of us on the desk. Suddenly he asked me about the rest of it; I denied any knowledge of its whereabouts. Had I been pressed I would have confessed at once, for I am no good at lying; this is one of my bad qualities: what my tongue hides my agitation betrays.

That which I feared had happened. The door was still locked and the neighbours, women and children, had gathered, nosing about for news of the incident. When the police broke into the flat they found on her bed the remains of Sheikha Madeeha, giving out a stench that caught at one's nose. My heart sank, my knees shook and I was overcome by a severe bout of dizziness. Composing myself, I became aware that everyone was blocking up his nose with his handkerchief or fingers, so I did likewise, and likewise I asked the same questions as they did: Did this mean there'd been a crime? And if there had been a crime, who were the accused, who the witnesses, and could it be that I would be a witness or an accused? And, if I were accused, what would the accusation amount to? Would it end up with my being found guilty?

The previous summer, at the beginning of the fourth and last year of my studies, I embarked with a broker upon looking for a room to shelter me. The first year I had been like a stray in the crush of Cairo; I had put up with my cousin, propping myself upon him while I sought to discover the secrets of the large city, stumbling around its twisted alleyways armed with my father's counsels and my mother's prayers and what little of their food and that of my brothers and sisters they made available to me. I discovered that my accent and the way I pronounced words would strip me bare before my Cairene fellow students, male and female. I discovered, to my amazement, that these men and women fellow students moved about together quite openly and without restriction, and I would have liked to behave likewise. However I lacked two things: the necessary talent or practice and a modicum of money. So I kept to myself and became withdrawn.

The previous summer my cousin got married. Returning from my village, I found his pretty young Cairene bride taking possession of the flat with smart and gleaming furniture, while my bed, chair, desk and books she had piled up in an out-of-the-way corner. So I went out in search of some place in which to shelter and eventually came across my room.

The previous summer I discovered that I was able, through the keyhole, to watch the women of the unassuming building as they hung out their washing: their own clothes and those of their husbands and children. Each Friday morning Madeeha would hang out her laundry. I noticed that she hung out only articles of female attire and that no men's or children's clothing was included. This was the second time I had made her acquaintance, the first being the day when I agreed with her, in her flat, to rent my room. On that day I had noted that she was in her forties and that her daughter, who was beside her, was in her twenties. When, though, she came to ask me about some washing of hers she had lost, she looked to be in her thirties. She was chewing gum and she assailed me with a scented and penetrating aroma; her dress was simple though of resplendent colours and had about it no affectation of modesty nor yet any violation of it; her words were few, spoken boldly yet politely. Even so I had the sensation that there was a secret call to me from her, a call that emanated from her perfume, her gum, her dress and her polite boldness. At night, while between sleep and wakefulness, I saw her parading before me, while the female fellow students whom I was in the habit of watching whenever overcome by sleeplessness at night had disappeared from sight.

On the second occasion I stood there for a long time while her daughter Zeinab was collecting up the washing. She enquired as to what was bothering me and I told her there was nothing wrong, although I had begun to think about what was in fact bothering me or about what I was perhaps in need of. My experience in the village and the district township first of all, then with my fellow students, male and female, at college, had taught me to fear and dread people; yet I do not learn. My need for others pushes me away from them.

Zeinab possessed neither the vivacity nor the attractiveness of her mother, though her youth gave out a quiet charm. I noticed that she would leave her home and return at different times of the day: sometimes at noon, sometimes in the evening, and some-times she would go out at night and not return before morning, for which I was able to find no explanation. However, I learned later that she worked as a nurse at a hospital. Her mother said casually: 'I do not fear for her, either from the ill or the healthy, be they doctors or male nurses, for, like her late father, she is emotionally tranquil, by which I mean frigid and rigid. Can you imagine that she passed through the state of adolescence as though she were an iceberg? Her husband can feel absolutely assured about his honour without the least expenditure of effort on his part. Ha! Ha! Ha! Zeinab has also inherited her looks, likewise her nature, from her late father. He died ten years ago and left me the girl, also this building, as my share of the estate and of the world.'

The girl's reticent behaviour seemed to me to be a silent protest at the mother's gaiety and unrestraint, and yet the tamed human being that was within her would change into a savage animal if she heard a bad word said against her mother. I heard her voice raised for the first time with one of the women living there as I went up the stairs on my way to my room, and I could not believe what I heard and saw – she was, to my utter surprise, defending my good name. For the first time I heard her pronouncing my name, and it seemed both to be and not to be my name: Maugoud Abdul Maugoud.

So they had begun to gossip. Perhaps they are prognosticating, for up till now nothing of what they suspect has occurred – and I trust that it won't. In any event, it was what I was expecting, what I was fearing; I was right in my expectation and what I feared occurred. I warned her but she did not heed my warning; her boldness frightens me and attracts me, drives me away and draws me close. It was an accusation that was both with and without foundation. She had paid me a visit in my room, a visit that appeared unintentional, and yet I know it could not have been other than intentional. It had been at dawn, before anyone comes up to the roof. But why should I seek to free myself of responsibility as though I had been chased and had been caught, without having myself made any effort, both more secretive and subtle than hers? I had forestalled her by passing by her and asking whether any letters had perhaps arrived from the country but had found Zeinab there instead of her; she had answered me briefly that nothing had arrived. However, I came back to the attack when the first of the month came, not to pay the rent, for the money hadn't yet arrived, but to apologize to her for not paying it, both wishing for and fearing her invitation. I was frightened of what other invitations would follow this one, and what gossip would follow such invitation. When I indicated to her that people's eyes were opened and that there was no point in having an accusation laid at our door of which we were innocent, her answer was a laugh, just as though I had made a joke.

How awe-inspiring is the female body! I am a village student at the local town school in the first class on the first day; I am the student from the provinces at Cairo University, the first moment on the first day. I must live with audacity and aloofness; I must learn and become accustomed; I must acquire something and some things must remain hidden within me. My teacher was capable and experienced, accustoming herself to the timorous wild animal. I would hear knocking at the door and it would spoil our enjoyment; I would find nothing but the wind and we would continue what had been interrupted, with me gliding down into magic caves, hiding my fear in the source of my fear.

The house overlooks a courtyard; in the courtyard celebrations for a saint's birthday are taking place. There are seventy thousand persons in the celebrations, each person has seventy thousand hands, in each hand there are seventy thousand slippers, in each slipper there are seventy thousand candles. They sway as they chant: 'The forbidden is done, destiny has been fulfilled. You are the all-forgiving.'

On the wedding day my books were moved from the top room to the bride's, while my dual-purpose furniture was kept in the room. I presented my bride with various modest gifts: a bottle of perfume, a dress and some red velvet slippers. The slippers were the cheapest of them and it was they which, to my astonishment, were the most admired. She hugged them to her and kissed them, and I now realize what an ill-omened prophecy your delight, O bride of mine, was bringing. As for my father, I was afraid to tell him.

The room had a door, the door a hole, the hole a key. She was careful to lock the door behind her with the key, and I was even more careful to keep the key in the keyhole, thus closing both it and Zeinab's eye if she wanted to peep in. Where is the place of refuge from people's eyes? We had closed the eyes of strangers only to open Zeinab's eyes.

Zeinab had the habit of carrying with her a duplicate of the key of the house to the different appointments her work took her to. After marrying she continued the practice, lest we awaken her doubts, she to whom the whisperings of people had reached. Leaving the key, the key of the door of the house with her, was our first line of defence. Leaving the key, the key of the door of the room, in its keyhole, was our second line of defence. The weak points in the two defences are evident: through the first you can be stolen up upon, through the second you can be surprised and brought to grief.

The slipper we found at the door of the room, while the wailing of women and the shrieks of children came from down in the lane. Guilty pleasure, and terror, rattled in the throat. So she had punctured the door with her ears; with them she had seen what we had hidden from her eyes. At the inquest it turned out that Zeinab had thrown herself over the wall, the roof wall, the roof on which was my room. Barefoot she lay, her eyes protruding, shocked by horror and the fall from such a height.

The secret of the slippers is known to no one but me and Madeeha. I tried to put them on my bride's foot while she was a corpse that we were consigning to the grave, but her mother, whose eyes gave out a ghastly glow, insisted on keeping them for herself. When the women mourners came, they found her hugging the slippers to her breast and kissing them.

On the following day she turned me out of her flat. I had intended to withdraw to my room at the top without waiting for any intimation from her. Her toughness scared me, her argument amazed me.

'Your wife has died and your continuance on your own in my flat is unacceptable on religious grounds.'

Feeling that I was being dilatory, she shouted:

'Go quietly or I'll call the police.'

Just as fear had brought me down, so fear took me up.

I got into the habit of tearing up my papers one after the other, my father's letters, the photos of the late Zeinab and her mother Madeeha, my teachers' notes; even my school books, and the notebooks in which I prepared my lectures for giving to the students, I got rid of, for there might be something in them which, without my knowing it, would convict me.

On the nights of the birthday celebrations Madeeha would go out, with dishevelled hair, bare of foot and wearing a tattered *galabia*. In each hand she would hold a slipper, in each slipper she would place a candle, on each candle she would make a flame. She would go on mumbling words, neither in a whisper nor shouting: 'Sins we committed and Your eye sleeps not. So, Lord of mankind, you have taken a terrible vengeance.' Then she would shriek: 'I saw you . . . I caught you . . . you and him.'

Ambiguity on lips of clarity; the secret is on the point of becoming a scandal. The deeper it penetrated into the lane, the higher it rose up into the building; it advanced a foot and went back a foot. The celebrations broke up with Madeeha still wandering round the streets. On her head was a tray, on the tray the two slippers, in the two slippers two candles, on the two candles two flames. The people were divided into two camps: one camp which, whenever they saw her, would marvel and admire, would stand in awe and ask her blessing, and another which, whenever they saw me – and without seeing me – would fabricate lies and whisper among themselves.

My fears were now concentrated on the two slippers, on their red colour, their velvet touch, and on the smell of feet and toes that lingered in them. In my sleep I saw them moving, as though some human being was wearing them, and they would freely roam around the walls of the room; whenever they reached the ceiling they would fall down on my head, and I would brush them away as I started up in fear, at which they would continue their journey. I would wake up to find that my bladder was filled with urine.

If I were to snatch them away, I would have snatched my secret away from the madwoman whose words were threatening me every day through what was being divulged, albeit not openly. More than once I made up my mind when we happened to meet, shambling through the dust of the lane in summer and wading through its slippery mud in winter, to attack her and wrest them from her, but I would fear my fear, the obscure would become clear, the secret exposed. Were she to leave them for an instant in her flat I would creep along to it and steal them, but she went out only with them, returned only with them.

One evening I knocked at her door. When she caught sight of me her eyes bulged, her voice became a hiss: 'Don't you dare come closer. I know why you've come.'

Then she hurried to her sofa that stood in the front room where the slippers lay; seizing them up, she hugged them to her, while I feigned calm in an attempt to calm her down too as she heard my reply:

'I have come to announce my renunciation of my share of the inheritance.'

'Liar.'

'And to announce that I have found another room.'

For a moment she was taken aback, then, waving the slippers, she said:

'You will not escape from the eye of God.'

She returned the slippers to her bosom, being careful to maintain the distance between herself and me, while I, studying the position, continued what I had to say:

'I came to pay off part of the debt I owe you.'

'You have many debts and are bankrupt.'

I stretched out my hand with the money and she stretched out a hand with which to take it, while the other held tight to both the slippers. This was my chance: these slippers were my secret and my enemy, my fear and my worry; it was I who had bought them, I who had made a present of them; they were thus from me and belonged to me. Why, then, should someone else be in possession of them so as to threaten me with them and to expose me? She pushed me in the chest with one hand, while her other held the slippers in a desperate grasp. How often had I kissed these two hands, tender and soft, and now one of them had sprouted the claws of a lioness defending her cub, while I caught sight of the swelling veins on the back of the other one as it was brought close up to my eyes, as though I were viewing it through a microscope; so close was it to my mouth that I was tempted to bite it, even to gnaw at it. It seemed, though, that there was no way for me to snatch away her charmed treasure merely by means of a localized battle of hands, especially as her shrieks were on the point of spoiling my plan. Strike the head and the hands will go limp. Had a second passed? Two seconds? The slippers were in my hands; my secret was mine. I locked the door behind me and hastened to my room. I was certain that no one had seen me, neither on the stairway nor on the roof. Here were the accursed slippers before me; I looked hard at them to make sure I really had them. I discovered, though – and what a terrible discovery it was – that I did not have their whole being, that a small piece of them, a piece, to be exact, of the right slipper at the back near the heel, had recently and remorselessly been snatched from it. Doubtless I had been forced, without noticing it, to leave it in her grasp as I hurried, frightened and joyful, from her flat, reckoning that my victory over her had been complete and that I had finally robbed her of her weapon against me. And yet here she was, still retaining, in her state of unconsciousness, a part of the whole I had reckoned was mine.

During my illness the two red slippers appeared anew to be chasing me round the walls of my room: once at dawn and again before evening set in. Despite the fact that I saw them with such clarity on both occasions that I could see where the piece had been wrenched from the right slipper, at the back exactly where the heel was, I realized that this could be as a result of the fever, a mere hallucination, and that I should cling to the factual evidence of my room: its walls, its tiled floor, its ceiling, the table and the sofa, the chair and the tumbler. I was frightened that I would lose contact with this world and never find my way back to it.

On that day I discovered that I had chosen cancer as a disease with which to frighten myself and of which to be frightened for those I loved. My choice of this disease was made because of the characteristics peculiar to it, it being almost the only malady for which medicine has as yet found neither cause nor cure; it attacks people of all ages; it sneaks up upon the body at any place, and any pain, even a mere upset without pain, is a warning of the onset of this malignant disease. As for the pain it gives, it is, in most cases, the most fearful and terrible.

That day my sensation of solitude was multiplied. That day I made two discoveries: the first of these was that I do not fear death, and the second was that not fearing death does not mean, as I had imagined, not fearing what comes before death. My fear of pain and of want, and of having my self-esteem slighted, became multiplied. That day I had been on the way to a quick recovery, except for the fact that the spectre of disease still terrifies me, and what terrifies me about it is that it will lead me to a world of illusions and hallucinations.

That day I discovered that my fears had extended so as to embrace all sides of my life: my fear that an illness will wholly cripple me, that my mother or father will die, that my head-master or inspector will write a bad report about me.

After being on my way to recovery I discovered that the illusion in my fears outstripped the reality: I had been ill and had recovered; my father had been exposed to an act of blood revenge in the village and had escaped unharmed; neither head-master nor inspector had done me wrong; and since the examining magistrate had released me a long time ago no person had entertained any doubts about me and no examining magistrate had detained or questioned me. I should, therefore, shake off my fear and proceed with confidence and equanimity. That day I ventured to visit a colleague of mine at his home and have my dinner at one of the city's most luxurious restaurants. On my return to my room I ventured to open the windows and, remov-ing the key from the keyhole, sank back, for the first time for many years, into a deep sleep without insomnia or anxiety, while moonlight and the night's breeze gently caressed me.

However, about a week after I was on my way to recovery, it happened that I received a telegram giving me the news of my father's death, suddenly and without warning. At that moment I was overcome by a deep feeling of regret; I realized that my fear for him had been protecting him and that I had preferred my own tranquillity and had abandoned my protection of him and that I had thus given death this golden opportunity to come upon me unawares and snatch him from me. Thus was I punished for my tranquillity, and that day I realized that my reward for my fear was that nothing I feared would take place – and if it did take place, its effect would be considerably less than expectations and imaginings had inflated it to.

From that day on, whenever I was tranquil I was frightened, and whenever I was frightened I was tranquil, and whenever I was tranquil I foresaw calamity, and whenever I was frightened I protected myself and was protected. From that day on I was disturbed when not finding something to disturb me.

When I hit her on the head she fell down in the middle of the hall. When I entered with the police her decomposed body was curled up on the sofa. The money she had taken from me at noon on Thursday was neither in her grasp nor yet scattered on the floor. After some days the medical report came stating that death had occurred on Friday morning. From that day on I moved between the middle of the hall and the sofa, between noon on Thursday and Friday morning. This was my place, this my time.

If the examining magistrate had for one moment doubted my words I would have told him everything and would have left it to him to define – in the light of the facts I supplied him with – the extent to which I was guilty or innocent, but I left everything suspended over my head, being neither innocent nor guilty. Thus what was hidden from me began to frighten me.

When I have an argument with a colleague or a boss I do not dare to allow the dispute to reach its limit and thus to become a quarrel or estrangement, for who knows, perhaps he has in some way come to know my disgraceful secret and will, in a moment, tear apart what the wall of fear has built up day by day, and bring down upon my head that with which I have protected myself for tens of years, ripping from me my masked face with which I have been screened, like the mother-of-pearl of sea-shells, like the tortoise's carapace, through a succession of nights and days, the passage of seconds and minutes, and would make it known that I was the object of suspicion where no suspicion lay. Thus I would quickly retreat before arousing his doubts so that he would burrow around in my past and so strike me at some mortal spot. I still remember the terror that came over me one day when I had a disagreement with a colleague and then learned that he had a relative who was living in the same lane as Sheikha Madeeha; so, although he made no reference during my quarrel to my problem, and although I made it up with him the following day, I took steps to be transferred from that town the same day on which we made it up, not resting till I was successful in my attempts.

That day I realized to what extent the nature of my personality had become dualistic by reason of the case against me, a dualism whose cancerous beginnings made their appearance at some unknown instant of my life's history, maybe the day I went down from my room to Sheikha Madeeha's flat, and it had no doubt deteriorated the day I stood before the examining magistrate and told him half the facts, hiding and denying the other half. And here I am today finding myself the victim of a bitter struggle between a belief I don't act upon and an action I don't believe in, and an embarrassment that is the more bitter because what I show is different from what I conceal within me.

When one evening I was visited by one of my relatives, a divorced woman who was hoping to marry me (while I, before her marriage and divorce, was contemplating marrying her), she revealed her charms with such a barefaced and unequivocal invitation that my desire was aroused. However, before making my advance to the final goal, my arousal abated when she looked at me – as I used to look at myself – with questioning perplexity. It was apparent to me that there was nothing to distract my attentions and that I was happy to receive such consideration and appreciation from a desirable female and that the least I could do was to reciprocate her appreciation. As for her, she dealt with the situation with superb adroitness, giving no sign that she was expecting more than this emotional closeness that expressed itself in whisperings and gropings. When alone with myself, however, I realized that Madeeha, Zeinab and the slippers, and those who were shouting, whispering and pointing, as also the examining magistrate, had all become deposited in my geological depths, practising from there the magical rites of my castration that I might be deprived of the rapture of sowing my seed and of the joy of reaping a harvest. What I had previously realized was now confirmed to me: that which I desire I do not achieve and that which I achieve I do not desire, and that between the desire that is not achieved and the achievement that is not desired falls my existence.

As for the thing I most fear, it is my succeeding or my excelling. During the past year all my students of all the years that I teach had passed, and I had been pleased both for my students and for myself. However, I soon discovered that I had committed a heinous crime, my colleagues accounting it a personal attack upon themselves, those nearest to me acting before those who were strangers to me. Perhaps they feared that their students would turn to me for private lessons and that I would thus deprive them of additional income, though I do not give such lessons unless it be for pressing reasons, in an irregular manner, and gratis – which, too, was something that upset them. They sent complaints to the headmaster of the school and to the district inspector, also to the Ministry of Education, accusing me of having given my students the questions before the examination. When I was interrogated it came out that it was not I who had set the examination and that I had had no knowledge of the questions. What, though, I was really afraid of was that one of them would scrutinize the layers of my past and discover my being accused in that case of mine, at which I would be irretrievably lost. From that day on I learned that I must stay in the shade, that I must not exhibit my enthusiasm or my sincerity, seeing that I was unable to give them up, and that I should hope that one or two of my students should fail if I wanted to be in the clear. However, that day too I realized to my great sorrow that my case was not subject to my will, for all my students might pass without my wanting them to and thus suspicion against me would again be resurrected. From that day on I no longer distinguished between right and wrong, realizing as I did that someone other than I was deciding for me, but without my being able to predict what punishment or reward I deserved.

When the examining magistrate allowed me to leave I did not believe him, his way of looking at me having been wholly one of suspicion. He was giving me the illusion of being free so as to obtain, from my behaviour and actions, evidence that would convict me, so let me be a thousand times more careful than him and not achieve for him what he wants.

The remains of the slippers I threw away that Thursday night, after loading them with stones, into a nearby canal of the Nile. They might float up at any moment – and with them my indictment; or a fisherman might rescue them and the investigation would be opened anew, the evidence showing that my neck deserved the hangman's noose, notwithstanding the truth which was known to no one, not even to myself.

I endeavoured to kill this moment of my life by various means, though I eventually discovered that I was killing only myself. I discovered, for instance, that those I knew at that time were composed of neighbours, friends and relatives, such as my cousin who had gone to the trouble of appointing a lawyer for me during the judicial enquiry, and I decided to avoid them altogether: let them consider me as dead and I them. I was successful in what I began but was surprised how it ended for me, for whenever I avoided contact with a neighbour, relative or friend, I felt that a part of my existence had fallen away, so that today I am scarcely acquainted with myself. The meaning of this is that, whenever I try to flee, I flee from myself rather than fleeing from my pursuer. My proof for this is that for many years I have been successful in avoiding all those who witnessed or heard about this case of mine, though I did, several days ago, meet up, to my horror, with my old examining magistrate, who, it appeared, had become an elderly and corpulent judge. Smartly dressed and smelling of after-shave, he was sitting in front of me in the dining-car of the train. Spotting me, he called out cheerfully: 'Any news about the Sheikha Madeeha case?' I tried to delude myself and others that the words were not addressed to me. His glances, though, were patently compromising and there was no way of escaping them. At that moment I discovered that my existence was recorded on my face, despite the moustache I had grown and my white hairs and wrinkles. Very abruptly – in order to avoid a scandal – I whispered: 'I don't know.'

In a singsong voice he went on:

'The important thing is the evidence. There is no value to what you denied during the investigation, nor even to what you may have confessed. A confession may have been extorted or it may have been motivated by the spirit of self-sacrifice in order to save some other person. Thus the lawyer is more important than the accused himself in determining the outcome of any case; the lawyer establishes or refutes the evidence despite the fact that the accused is his own first witness. The important thing . . .'

As though we were an orchestra, I joined in with him in finishing the sentence:

'. . . is the evidence.'

I took courage and asked him with disguised cunning:

'So they're still waiting for . . . the evidence?'

Continuing his song, he answered me:

'The file still exists, even though the examining magistrate has changed, awaiting any addition, however distant in time or place.'

I knew what his reply would be before he uttered it; it was just like someone seeking confirmation of something he knows, yet his answer terrified me. And so – and lest he start singing anew – I decided to make another enquiry of him. He, though, was determined to continue to interrogate me: And where, God permitting, was I bound for? For an instant I thought of concealing this from him, but I was frightened that his station might be after mine and that my lie would be discovered and I would thus be led to certain doom. There was therefore nothing for it but to admit to my true destination, after which I tried to avoid conversing with him, though he would from time to time terrify me with a question connected, or unconnected, with my case.

I gave up my old friends and took in their place one single friend who would stand as a wall between me and my past; in him I would protect myself and in him I would hide myself. However,

I discovered one day that he knew my old examining magistrate, who was both his relative and neighbour. He might mention my name in front of him by chance, just as he had mentioned his name in front of me, and would relate my story to him, thus destroying that by which I tried to protect myself from him and so would fall into what I had tried to escape from, for were it not for my friendship with him it would not be likely that his tongue would let slip my name. From that day on I realized that as the number of my friends increased so too did the probabilities of my being accused, for I did not know which of them was in contact with my old examining magistrate, nor which of them was the object of some old suspicion. All of which led me to believe that there was no way of escaping the fact that my life was my suffering and that my mere existence was the quintessence of my tragedy.

The thing that most upset me was when my friend decided to be hospitable just when I had made up my mind to break with him. One day he invited me to a party at his house and from what he said I understood that my old examining magistrate would be among those invited. While I was trembling in terror, my friend no doubt was thinking how much I was welcoming the opportunity of making the acquaintance of men of influence and enjoying seeing beautiful, smartly dressed women and gay, elegant young ladies, breathing in their fragrance, and being intoxicated by their laughter. For this reason my friend did not comprehend – and he would never be able to do so – the deep, bottomless expression of melancholy that appeared on my face. Owing to my great distress I was not afforded the necessary suavity or courage to make my apologies. When the date of the party came, however, I told myself that I was certainly too ill to accept my friend's invitation, and so I laid low in my room, determined in future to avoid my friend as much as possible lest he expose me unwittingly to even more dangerous predicaments. If I had succeeded in making good my escape this time, who knows whether I'd be able to do so on the next occasion. No doubt my friend found no explanation for my behaviour, which completely took him aback, perhaps for a long time.

One day I was giving a lecture on psychology when a student surprised me with the question: Is nostalgia for the mother's womb or the desire to return to the foetal stage (page sixty-one of the set book) a defence of the self or an extermination of it? Whereas I was accustomed to having misgivings about the questions some of my spiteful students would pose, this question, unusually, so stirred my deep feelings of sadness that I almost wept – especially as I had not prepared myself to answer it.

When my inspector came to write his report on me he was laughing confidently. I repeated to him the student's question:

'Is craving for the mother's womb a defence of the self or an extermination of it?'

His face suddenly took on an expression of dejection and he whispered:

'Look, my son, it is a defence of the self and ends with its extermination.'

He was a sympathetic and understanding inspector, differing from the rest of the inspectors and headmasters with whom I worked. Perhaps he was speaking from some experience through which he had lived and not from the pages of the set book. I was thus not worried about what he might have written about me in his report.

And now night comes and I securely bolt my windows, block up the keyhole with the key as I used to do of old. I do not learn and do not change. I sleep in a squatting position as the foetus sleeps in its mother's belly. How terrified I am of the night, of the gloom of night! How terrible is sleeplessness and anxiety in my room!

It is my fortress and my snare. I know it now with all my senses: the colour of its walls, its windows, its tiled floor, that part of it that has remained constant and that which has changed, its cobwebby corners up by the ceiling, its dusty corners down on the floor; its smell when it has been locked up for a long time, and when I cook my food in it, and when I open the adjoining lavatory. I even know the taste and touch of the lower parts of its walls: white, crumbly and salty. Daily they grow thinner and I am terrified that one day I shall find they have been completely corroded and that thus all my plans will collapse from their very foundation. As for its sounds, I am wholly familiar with them:

wary, mysterious sounds. What terrifies me about them is that they issue from unknown places. An attempt at defining them puts me at ease: perhaps a mouse gnawing at remains of food in the rubbish bin or a cockroach amusing itself merrily in the lavatory. Then there are other noises, distant or close, above or below, that grow in volume in the darkness and stillness of night: two cats wooing or yowling, a dog barking, a foot treading, things breaking. Just as I have become fond of my room, it in its turn must have become accustomed to me: my heartbeats when they grow so loud that they resemble the beating of a drum, and when they grow so soft that they come almost to a stop; my breathing when it goes fast and then slow; it is, too, the witness to my sleeplessness and my anxiety, and to the fact that I enter it on my return from work and do not leave it again till the following morning, as also to the fact that I neither pay visits nor am visited.

And so, for the sake of maintaining my freedom, I put obstacles in its way. I myself have interned myself that I may save someone the effort of interning me, and my password being in my own hand is better than its being in someone else's, or in his grasp or fist.

Postscript
By virtue of my studies – and sometimes as a hobby – I have read fiction. As for my own experiences with writing, they are confined to the demands made of me by my professors and the letters I used to write to my father, may the Lord now rest his soul. This was my only experience in the realm of writing, and so it is that while I am the originator of this story I am not its author. Its author is the person whose name is given alongside the title, for I am not so stupid as to record against myself words that, while possibly indicating my innocence, could equally well point to my guilt. I have thus concealed both my age and my address, while my name and occupation are both made up. Those means of access to my personality I have blocked up in the same way as I blocked up of old the keyhole with the key. I am not a lover of fiction nor a seeker after glory; everything which tends to reveal me I am apprehensive about, for it could be a piece of evidence

against me to be added to my records. At school parties I am nonplussed by colleagues who vie with one another to be in the limelight by making a speech or supervising the activities of their students and I would point to them pityingly: there they were, condemning their own selves. For this reason I make a point of sitting in the back rows and when the cameramen come along I'm careful to hide my face behind the man or woman sitting in front of me so that my presence will not be recorded and become evidence against me one of these days. However, on looking at one of these photographs, I found that I had hidden my face in a quite obvious manner so that anyone seeing it would discover what I was attempting should not be discovered, and so I realized that if my face exposed me to being suspected, my hiding it exposed me to being suspected even more. So I withdrew myself far away from the eyes and ears and noses of others, for my mere presence in a spacious and crowded place is an announcement of myself and a raising of the doubts that follow such an announcement. Thus it confuses and oppresses me to sit at a café or in a club where there are bleary eyes that scan and scrutinize me, assault and paralyse me, and where there are loitering ears that may hunt down some suspicion or semi-suspicion, and where there are always those who feel me out and smell me out, whereas I find others conversing and shouting and playing and clapping and guffawing and drinking and eating and coming and going, and I ask myself which of them are the accused and which the witnesses, which the convicted and which the judges, the examining magistrates and the prosecutors, and which are like me, neither accused nor innocent nor guilty. And so success and fame and everything that people imagine brings joy to others is to me a source of deep sadness and despondency.

Every year I say: 'This is the last birthday for you to celebrate before life is wiped out for you, without rites or ceremony.' Every month I say: 'This is the last salary you will receive before the man that you have become is annihilated as a punishment for the adolescent that you were.' Every week I say: 'This is the last time you will take a bath before you are found guilty because of what you have striven to extricate yourself from and which, it has seemed to them, you have sunk deeper into.' And every day when I shave I say: 'This is the last morning you will see your room before they break in upon your privacy.' And every year, and every month, and every week and every day I find myself existing and I thank God because I am still breathing in the walls of my room, utterly unable to predict my fate the next instant, and the instant after the next. Whenever I celebrate my birthday, and receive my salary, and have a bath and shave, I say: 'Now you have become ready to meet the moment that is coming and doesn't come and yet will come.' Thus at every turn of time my fear renews its youth; it neither rusts nor abates.

But even if I am able to succeed in maintaining seclusion in my room, I well realize that my existence, which started at the first word on the first line, has almost come to its end . . . I become a mere memory which has for several moments become known, as though, while an earthquake is taking place, or an air-raid, or the investigation of a serious crime, it will after a while, be it long or short, lose itself in the crush of the living and the dead.

Postscript
I am frightened, therefore I am non-existent.

ALIFA RIFAAT

Another Evening at the Club

In a state of tension, she awaited the return of her husband. At a loss to predict what would happen between them, she moved herself back and forth in the rocking chair on the wide wooden verandah that ran along the bank and occupied part of the river itself, its supports being fixed in the river bed, while around it grew grasses and reeds. As though to banish her apprehension, she passed her fingers across her hair. The spectres of the eucalyptus trees ranged along the garden fence rocked before her gaze, with white egrets slumbering on their high branches like huge white flowers among the thin leaves.

The crescent moon rose from behind the eastern mountains and the peaks of the gently stirring waves glistened in its feeble rays, intermingled with threads of light leaking from the houses of Manfalout scattered along the opposite bank. The coloured bulbs fixed to the trees in the garden of the club at the far end of the town stood out against the surrounding darkness. Somewhere over there her husband now sat, most likely engrossed in a game of chess.

It was only a few years ago that she had first laid eyes on him at her father's house, meeting his gaze that weighed up her beauty and priced it before offering the dowry. She had noted his eyes ranging over her as she presented him with the coffee in the Japanese cups that were kept safely locked away in the cupboard for important guests. Her mother had herself laid them out on the silver-plated tray with its elaborately embroidered spread. When the two men had taken their coffee, her father had looked up at her with a smile and had told her to sit down, and she had seated herself on the sofa facing them, drawing the end of her dress over her knees and looking through lowered lids at the man

68

who might choose her as his wife. She had been glad to see that he was tall, well-built and clean-shaven except for a thin greying moustache. In particular she noticed the well-cut coat of English tweed and the silk shirt with gold links. She had felt herself blushing as she saw him returning her gaze. Then the man turned to her father and took out a gold case and offered him a cigarette.

'You really shouldn't, my dear sir,' said her father, patting his chest with his left hand and extracting a cigarette with trembling fingers. Before he could bring out his box of matches Abboud Bey had produced his lighter.

'No, after you, my dear sir,' said her father in embarrassment. Mingled with her sense of excitement at this man who gave out such an air of worldly self-confidence was a guilty shame at her father's inadequacy.

After lighting her father's cigarette Abboud Bey sat back, crossing his legs, and took out a cigarette for himself. He tapped it against the case before putting it in the corner of his mouth and lighting it, then blew out circles of smoke that followed each other across the room.

'It's a great honour for us, my son,' said her father, smiling first at Abboud Bey, then at his daughter, at which Abboud Bey looked across at her and asked:

'And the beautiful little girl's still at secondary school?'

She lowered her head modestly and her father had answered:

'As from today she'll be staying at home in readiness for your happy life together, Allah permitting,' and at a glance from her father she had hurried off to join her mother in the kitchen.

'You're a lucky girl,' her mother had told her. 'He's a real find. Any girl would be happy to have him. He's an Inspector of Irrigation though he's not yet forty. He earns a big salary and gets a fully furnished government house wherever he's posted, which will save us the expense of setting up a house – and I don't have to tell you what our situation is – and that's besides the house he owns in Alexandria where you'll be spending your holidays.'

Samia had wondered to herself how such a splendid suitor had found his way to her door. Who had told him that Mr Mahmoud Barakat, a mere clerk at the Court of Appeal, had a beautiful daughter of good reputation?

The days were then taken up with going the rounds of Cairo's shops and choosing clothes for the new grand life she would be living. This was made possible by her father borrowing on the security of his government pension. Abboud Bey, on his part, never visited her without bringing a present. For her birthday, just before they were married, he bought her an emerald ring that came in a plush box bearing the name of a well-known jeweller in Kasr el-Nil Street. On her wedding night, as he put a diamond bracelet round her wrist, he had reminded her that she was marrying someone with a brilliant career in front of him and that one of the most important things in life was the opinion of others, particularly one's equals and seniors. Though she was still only a young girl she must try to act with suitable dignity.

'Tell people you're from the well-known Barakat family and that your father was a judge,' and he went up to her and gently patted her cheeks in a fatherly, reassuring gesture that he was often to repeat during their times together.

Then, yesterday evening, she had returned from the club somewhat light-headed from the bottle of beer she had been required to drink on the occasion of someone's birthday. Her husband, noting the state she was in, hurriedly took her back home. She had undressed and put on her nightgown, leaving her jewellery on the dressing-table, and was fast asleep seconds after getting into bed. The following morning, fully recovered, she slept late, then rang the bell as usual and had breakfast brought to her. It was only as she was putting her jewellery away in the wooden and mother-of-pearl box that she realized her emerald ring was missing.

Could it have dropped from her finger at the club? In the car on the way back? No, she distinctly remembered it last thing at night, remembered the usual difficulty she had in getting it off her finger. She stripped the bed of its sheets, turned over the mattress, looked inside the pillow cases, crawled on hands and knees under the bed. The tray of breakfast lying on the small bedside table caught her eye and she remembered the young servant coming in that morning with it, remembered the noise of the tray being put down, the curtains being drawn, the tray then being lifted up again and placed on the bedside table. No one but the servant had entered the room. Should she call her and question her?

Eventually, having taken two aspirins, she decided to do nothing and await the return of her husband from work.

Directly he arrived she told him what had happened and he took her by the arm and seated her down beside him:

'Let's just calm down and go over what happened.'

She repeated, this time with further details, the whole story.

'And you've looked for it?'

'Everywhere. Every possible and impossible place in the bedroom and the bathroom. You see, I remember distinctly taking it off last night.'

He grimaced at the thought of last night, then said:

'Anybody been in the room since Gazia when she brought in the breakfast?'

'Not a soul. I've even told Gazia not to do the room today.'

'And you've not mentioned anything to her?'

'I thought I'd better leave it to you.'

'Fine, go and tell her I want to speak to her. There's no point in your saying anything but I think it would be as well if you were present when I talk to her.'

Five minutes later Gazia, the young servant girl they had recently employed, entered behind her mistress. Samia took herself to a far corner of the room while Gazia stood in front of Abboud Bey, her hands folded across her chest, her eyes lowered.

'Yes, sir?'

'Where's the ring?'

'What ring are you talking about, sir?'

'Now don't make out you don't know. The one with the green stone. It would be better for you if you hand it over and then nothing more need be said.'

'May Allah blind me if I've set eyes on it.'

He stood up and gave her a sudden slap on the face. The girl reeled back, put one hand to her cheek, then lowered it again to her chest and made no answer to any of Abboud's questions. Finally he said to her:

'You've got just fifteen seconds to say where you've hidden the ring or else, I swear to you, you're not going to have a good time of it.'

As he lifted up his arm to look at his watch the girl flinched slightly but continued in her silence. When he went to the telephone Samia raised her head and saw that the girl's cheeks were wet with tears. Abboud Bey got through to the Superintendent of Police and told him briefly what had occurred.

'Of course I haven't got any actual proof but seeing that no one else entered the room, it's obvious she's pinched it. Anyway I'll leave the matter in your capable hands – I know your people have their ways and means.'

He gave a short laugh, then listened for a while and said: 'I'm really most grateful to you.'

He put down the receiver and turned round to Samia:

'That's it, my dear. There's nothing more to worry about. The Superintendent has promised me we'll get it back. The patrol car's on the way.'

The following day, in the late afternoon, she'd been sitting in front of her dressing-table rearranging her jewellery in its box when an earring slipped from her grasp and fell to the floor. As she bent to pick it up she saw the emerald ring stuck between the leg of the table and the wall. Since that moment she had sat in a state of panic awaiting her husband's return from the club. She even felt tempted to walk down to the water's edge and throw it into the river so as to be rid of the unpleasantness that lay ahead.

At the sound of the screech of tyres rounding the house to the garage, she slipped the ring on to her finger. As he entered she stood up and raised her hand to show him the ring. Quickly, trying to choose her words but knowing that she was expressing herself clumsily, she explained what an extraordinary thing it was that it should have lodged itself between the dressing-table and the wall, what an extraordinary coincidence she should have dropped the earring and so seen it, how she'd thought of ringing him at the club to tell him the good news but . . .

She stopped in mid-sentence when she saw his frown and added weakly: 'I'm sorry. I can't think how it could have happened. What do we do now?'

He shrugged his shoulders as though in surprise.

'Are you asking me, my dear lady? Nothing of course.'

'But they've been beating up the girl – you yourself said they'd

72

not let her be till she confessed.'

Unhurriedly, he sat himself down as though to consider this new aspect of the matter. Taking out his case, he tapped a cigarette against it in his accustomed manner, then moistened his lips, put the cigarette in place and lit it. The smoke rings hovered in the still air as he looked at his watch and said:

'In any case she's not got all that long before they let her go. They can't keep her for more than forty-eight hours without getting any evidence or a confession. It won't kill her to put up with things for a while longer. By now the whole town knows the servant stole the ring – or would you like me to tell everyone: "Look, folks, the fact is that the wife got a bit tiddly on a couple of sips of beer and the ring took off on its own and hid itself behind the dressing-table."? What do you think?'

'I know the situation's a bit awkward . . .'

'Awkward? It's downright ludicrous. Listen, there's nothing to be done but to give it to me and the next time I go down to Cairo I'll sell it and get something else in its place. We'd be the laughing-stock of the town.'

He stretched out his hand and she found herself taking off the ring and placing it in the outstretched palm. She was careful that their eyes should not meet. For a moment she was on the point of protesting and in fact uttered a few words:

'I'd just like to say we could . . .'

Putting the ring away in his pocket, he bent over her and with both hands gently patted her on the cheeks. It was a gesture she had long become used to, a gesture that promised her continued security, that told her that this man who was her husband and the father of her child had also taken the place of her father who, as though assured that he had found her a suitable substitute, had followed up her marriage with his own funeral. The gesture told her more eloquently than any words that he was the man, she the woman, he the one who carried the responsibilities, made the decisions, she the one whose role it was to be beautiful, happy, carefree. Now, though, for the first time in their life together the gesture came like a slap in the face.

Directly he removed his hands her whole body was seized with an uncontrollable trembling. Frightened he would notice, she rose to her feet and walked with deliberate steps towards the large window. She leaned her forehead against the comforting cold surface and closed her eyes tightly for several seconds. When she opened them she noticed that the café lights strung between the trees on the opposite shore had been turned on and that there were men seated under them and a waiter moving among the tables. The dark shape of a boat momentarily blocked out the café scene; in the light from the hurricane lamp hanging from its bow she saw it cutting through several of those floating islands of Nile waterlilies that, rootless, are swept along with the current.

Suddenly she became aware of his presence alongside her.

'Why don't you go and change quickly while I take the car out? It's hot and it would be nice to have supper at the club.'

'As you like. Why not?'

By the time she had turned round from the window she was smiling.

TAYEB SALIH

The Cypriot Man

Nicosia in July was as though Khartoum had been transplanted to Damascus. The streets, as laid out by the British, were broad, the desert was that of Khartoum, but there was that struggle between the east and west winds that I remember in Damascus.

It was British from head to toe, despite all that blood that had been spilt. I was surprised for I had expected a town of Greek character. The man, though, did not give me time to pursue my thought to its conclusion but came and sat himself beside me at the edge of the swimming-pool. He made a slight gesture with his head and they brought him a cup of coffee.

'Tourist?' he said.

'Yes.'

He made a noise the import of which I did not follow – it was as though he were saying that the likes of me didn't deserve to be a tourist in Nicosia, or that Nicosia didn't deserve to have the likes of me being a tourist in it.

I turned my attention from him so as to examine a woman with a face like that of one of Raphael's angels, and a body like that of Gauguin's women. Was she the wife or the other woman? Again he cut through the thread of my thoughts:

'Where are you from?'

'The Sudan.'

'What do you do?'

'I'm in government service.'

I laughed for in fact I didn't work for the government; anyway governments have broad shoulders.

'I don't work,' he said. 'I own a factory.'

'Really?'

'For making women's clothes.'

75

'How lovely.'

'I've made a lot of money. I worked like a black. I made a fortune. I don't work any longer – spend all my time in bed.'

'Sleeping?'

'You must be joking. What does a man do in bed?'

'Don't you get tired?'

'You're joking. Look at me – what age do you think I am?'

Sometimes fifty, sometimes seventy, but I didn't want to encourage him.

'Seventy,' I said to him.

This did not upset him as I had presumed. He gave a resounding laugh and said:

'Seventy-five in actual fact, but no one takes me for more than fifty. Go on, be truthful.'

'All right, fifty.'

'Why do you think it is?'

'Because you take exercise.'

'Yes, in bed, I bash away – white and black, red and yellow: all colours. Europeans, negresses, Indians, Arabs, Jewesses; Muslims, Christians, Buddhists: all religions.'

'You're a liberal-minded man.'

'Yes, in bed.'

'And outside.'

'I hate Jews.'

'Why do you hate Jews?'

'Just so. Also they play with skill.'

'What?'

'The game of death. They've been at it for centuries.'

'Why does that make you angry?'

'Because I . . . because I . . . it's of no consequence.'

'Are they not defeated?'

'They all give up in the end.'

'And their women?'

'There's no one better than them in bed. The greater your hatred for them, the greater your enjoyment with their women. They are my chosen people.'

'And the negroes of America?'

'My relationship with them has not reached the stage of hatred. I must pay them more attention.'

76

'And the Arabs?'

'They provoke laughter or pity. They give up easily, these days anyway. Playing with them is not enjoyable because it's one-sided.'

I thought: if only they had accepted Cyprus, if only Balfour had promised them it.

The Cypriot man gave his resounding laugh and said:

'Women prolong one's life. A man must appear to be at least twenty years younger than he is. That's what being smart is.'

'Do you fool death?'

'What is death? Someone you meet by chance, who sits with you as we are sitting now, who talks freely with you, perhaps about the weather or women or shares on the stock market. Then he politely sees you to the door. He opens the door and signs for you to go out. After that you don't know.'

A grey cloud stayed overhead for a while, but at that moment I did not know that the divining arrows had been cast and that the Cypriot man was playing a hazardous game with me.

The wave of laughter broadened out and enfolded me. They were a sweet family which I had come to like since sitting down: the father with his good-natured face and the mother with her English voice which was like an Elizabethan air played on the strings of an ancient lyre, and four daughters, the eldest of whom was not more than twelve, who would go in and out of the pool, laughing and teasing their parents. They would smile at me and broaden the compass of their happiness till it included me. There came a moment when I saw on the father's face that he was about to invite me to join them; it was at that moment that the Cypriot man descended upon me. The eldest girl got up and stepped gracefully towards the pool. With the girl having suddenly come to a stop as though some mysterious power had halted her, the Cypriot man said:

'This one I'd pay a hundred pounds sterling for.'

'What for?' I said to him in alarm.

The Cypriot man made an obscene gesture with his arm.

At that moment the girl fell face-down on to the stone and blood poured from her forehead. The good-natured family started up, like frightened birds, and surrounded the girl. I immediately got up from beside the man, feeling for him an overwhelming hatred, and seated myself at a table far away from him. I remembered my own daughters and their mother in Beirut and was angry. I saw the members of the delightful family making their departures, sadly, the daughters clinging to their mother, the mother reproaching the father, and I became more angry. Then I quietened down and the things around me quietened down. The clamour died away and there came to me my friend Taher Wad Rawwasi and sat beside me: on the bench in front of Sa'eed's shop. His face was beaming, full of health and energy.

'Really,' I said to him, 'why is it that you haven't grown old and weak though you're older than all of them?'

'From when I first became aware of the world,' he said, 'I've been on the move. I don't remember ever not moving. I work like a horse and if there's no work to be done I create something to busy myself with. I go to sleep at any old time, early or late, and wake up directly the *muezzin* says "God is great, God is great" for the dawn prayer.'

'But you don't pray?'

'I say the *shahada*[1] and ask God's forgiveness after the *muezzin* has finished giving the call to prayers, and my heart finds assurance that the world is going along as it always has. I take a nap for half an hour or so. The odd thing is that a nap after the call to prayers is for me equal to the whole night's sleep. After that I wake up as though I've been woken by an alarm clock. I make the tea and wake Fatima up. She performs the dawn prayer. We drink tea. I go down to meet the sun on the Nile's surface and say to God's morning Hello and Welcome. However long I'm away I come back to find the breakfast ready. We sit down to it, Fatima and I and any of God's servants that destiny brings to us. For more than fifty years it's been like this.'

One day I'll ask Taher Wad Rawwasi about the story of his marriage to Fatima bint Jabr ad-Dar, one of Mahjoub's four sisters. His loyalty was not to himself but to Mahjoub, and he used to make fun both of himself and of the world. Would he become a hero? It was clear that if it really came to it he would sacrifice himself for Mahjoub. Should I ask him now? However, off his own bat, he uttered a short phrase compounded of the fabric of his whole life:

'Fatima bint Jabr ad-Dar – what a girl!'

'And Mahjoub?'

Taher Wad Rawwasi gave a laugh that had the flavour of those bygone days; it indicated the extent of his love for Mahjoub. Even mentioning his name would fill him with happiness, as though the presence of Mahjoub on the face of the earth made it less hostile, better, in Taher Wad Rawwasi's view. He laughed and said, laughing:

'Mahjoub's something else; Mahjoub's made of a different clay.'

Then he fell silent and it was clear to me that he didn't, at that time, wish to say any more on that particular subject. After a time I asked him:

'Abdul Hafeez said you'd never in your whole life entered a mosque. Is that so?'

'Just once I entered a mosque.'

'Why? What for?'

'Only the once. It was one winter, in *Touba* or *Amsheer,*[2] God knows best.'

'It was in *Amsheer,*' I said to him, 'after you'd buried Maryam at night.'

'That's right. How did you know?'

'I was there with you.'

'Where? I didn't see you that morning, though the whole village had collected on that day in the mosque.'

'I was by the window, appearing and disappearing till you said "And not those who are astray. Amen." '[3]

'And then?'

'God be praised. Poor Meheimeed was calling out "Where's the man who was here gone to?" '

'And then?'

Suddenly the dream bird flew away. Wad Rawwasi disappeared, as did Wad Hamid[4] with all its probabilities. Where he had been sitting I saw the Cypriot man, I heard his voice and my heart contracted. I heard his shouting and the hubbub, the slapping of the water against the sides of the swimming-pool, with spectres shaped in the form of naked women and naked men and children leaping about and shrieking. The voice was saying:

'For this one I'd only pay fifty pounds sterling.'

I pressed down on my eyes so as to be more awake. I looked at the goods on offer in the market. It was that woman. She was drinking orange juice at the moment at which the Cypriot man had said what he did. She spluttered and choked; a man leapt to his feet to help her, then a woman; servants and waiters came along, people gathered, and they carried her off unconscious. It was as if a magician had waved his wand and, so it seemed to me, the people instantly vanished; and the darkness too, as though close at hand, awaiting a signal from someone, came down all at once. The Cypriot man and I on our own with the light playing around on the surface of the water. Between the light and the darkness he said to me:

'Two American girls arrived this morning from New York. They're very beautiful, very rich. One's eighteen and she's mine; the other's twenty-five and she's for you. They're sisters; they own a villa in Kyrenia. I've got a car. The adventure won't cost you a thing. Come along. They'll be really taken by your colour.'

The darkness and the light were wrestling around the swimming-pool, while it was as if the voice of the Cypriot man were supplying the armies of darkness with weapons. Thus I wanted to say to him All right, but another sound issued from my throat involuntarily, and I said to him, as I followed the war taking place on the water's surface:

'No, thank you. I didn't come to Nicosia in search of that. I came to have a quiet talk with my friend Taher Wad Rawwasi because he refused to visit me in London and I failed to meet him in Beirut.'

Then I turned to him – and what a ghastly sight met my eyes. Was I imagining things, or dreaming, or mad? I ran, ran to take refuge with the crowd in the hotel bar. I asked for something to drink; I drank it, without recollecting the taste of it or what it was. I calmed down a little. But the Cypriot man came and sat down with me. He had bounded along on crutches. He asked for whisky, a double. He said that he had lost his right leg in the war. What war? One of the wars, what did it matter which one? His wooden leg had been smashed this morning. He had climbed up a mountain. He was waiting for a new leg from London. Sometimes his voice was English, sometimes it had a German accent; at others it seemed French to me; he used American words.

'Are you . . .'

'No, I'm not. Some people think I'm Italian, some that I'm Russian; others German . . . Spanish. Once an American tourist asked me whether I was from Basutoland. Just imagine. What's it matter where I'm from? And Your Excellency?'

'Why do you say to me Your Excellency?'

'Because you're a very fine person.'

'And what's my importance?'

'You exist today and you won't exist tomorrow – and you won't recur.'

'That happens to every person – what's important about that?'

'Not every person is aware of it. You, Excellency, are aware of your position in time and place.'

'I don't believe so.'

He put down his drink in one gulp and stood up, on two sound legs, unless I was imagining things, or was dreaming or mad, and it was as though he were the Cypriot man. He bowed with very affected politeness, and it was as though his face as I had seen it at the edge of the pool made you sense that life had no value.

'I won't say goodbye,' he said, 'but *au revoir*, Excellency.'

It was ten o'clock when I went to bed. I did everything possible to bring sleep about, being tired and having swum all day. I tried talking to Taher Wad Rawwasi. I asked him about the story of his marriage to Fatima bint Jabr ad-Dar. I asked him about his attendance at dawn prayers on that memorable day. I asked him about that singing which was linking the two banks with silken threads, while poor Meheimeed was floundering about in the waves in pursuit of Maryam's phantom, but he did not reply. Music was of no help to me, neither was reading. I could have gone out, gone to a night club or for a walk, or I could have sat in the hotel bar. There was nothing I could do. Then the pain began: a slight numbness at the tips of the toes which gradually began to advance upwards until it was as though terrible claws were tearing at my stomach, chest, back and head: the fires of hell had all at once broken out.

I would lose consciousness then enter into a terrible vortex of pains and fires; the frightful face would show itself to me between unconsciousness and a state of semi-wakefulness, leaping from chair to chair, disappearing and reappearing all over the room. Voices I did not understand came to me from the unknown, faces I did not know, dark and scowling. There was nothing I could do. Though in some manner in a state of consciousness, I was incapable of lifting up the receiver and calling a doctor, or going down to reception in the hotel, or crying out for help. There was a savage and silent war taking place between me and unknown fates. I certainly gained some sort of a victory, for I came to to the sound of four o'clock in the morning striking, with the hotel and the town silent. The pains had gone except for a sensation of exhaustion and overwhelming despair, as though the world, the good and the evil of it, were not worth a gnat's wing. After that I slept. At nine o'clock in the morning the plane taking me to Beirut circled above Nicosia; it looked to me like an ancient cemetery.

On the evening of the following day in Beirut the doorbell rang. It was a woman clad in black carrying a child. She was crying and the first sentence she said was:

'I'm Palestinian – my daughter has died.'

I stood for a while looking at her, not knowing what to say; however, she entered, sat down and said:

'Will you let me rest and feed my child?'

While she was telling me her story the doorbell rang. I took a telegram and opened it, with the Palestinian woman telling me her formidable misfortune, while I was engrossed in my own.

I crossed seas and deserts, wanting to know before all else when and how he had died. They informed me that he had as usual worked in the garden in his field in the morning and had done those things he usually did during his day. He had not complained of anything. He had entered his relations' homes, sat with his friends here and there; he'd brought some half-ripe dates and drunk coffee with them. My name had cropped up in his conversation several times. He had been awaiting my arrival impatiently, for I had written to him that I was coming. He supped lightly as usual, performed the evening prayer, then about ten o'clock the harbingers of death had come to him; before the dawn prayer he had departed this world, and when the aeroplane was bearing me from Nicosia to Beirut they had just finished burying him.

At forenoon I stood by his grave, with the Cypriot man sitting at the side of the grave, in his formal guise, listening to me as I gave prayers and supplications. He said to me in a voice that seemed to issue from the earth and the sky, encompassing me from all sides:

'You won't see me again in this guise other than at the last moment when I shall open the door to you, bow quietly and say to you "After you, Your Excellency." You will see me in other and various guises. You may encounter me in the form of a beautiful girl, who will come to you and tell you she admires your views and opinions and that she'd like to do an interview with you for some paper or magazine; or in the shape of a president or a ruler who offers you some post that makes your heart lose a beat; or in the form of one of life's pranks that gives you a lot of money without your expending any effort; perhaps in the form of a vast multitude that applauds you for some reason you don't know; or perhaps you'll see me in the form of a girl twenty years younger than you, whom you desire and who'll say to you: "Let's go to an isolated hut way up in the mountains." Beware. Your father will not be there on the next occasion to give his life for you. Beware. The term of life is designated, but we take into consideration the skill shown in playing the game. Beware for you are now ascending towards the mountain peak.'

Notes
1. The doctrinal formula of Islam: 'There is no god but God and Mohammed is the Messenger of God.'
2. Winter months in the Coptic calendar.
3. The final words of the *Fatiha*, the equivalent in Islam of the Lord's Prayer.
4. The village in which most of the writer's novels and short stories are placed.

IBRAHIM AL-KOUNI

The Drumming Sands

Misbah Said jumped down from the Land-Rover and took out a
blanket and spread it under a sparse desert tree. He watched his
companion opening the front of the Land-Rover, examining the
oil and letting the motor cool off. He gave an encompassing look
at the emptiness, silent and surrendered to the sun, while the
sound of the engine still buzzed in his ears. 'Jabbour', he said,
collapsing on to the blanket, 'you wouldn't have an Aspro, would
you? The noise of your car has given me a headache.' He spat on
to the sands that glistened under the sun's rays and watched the
spittle disappear into the thirsty pores.

'I feel my brain's boiling,' he added.

Jabbour approached with a loaf of bread, tins of sardines and a
bottle filled with a yellow-coloured liquid.

'You people of the city aren't used to the desert. Wait, I've got
nature's cure for headaches and all other illnesses, a medicine a
lot more effective than Aspro.'

'Whiskey in this heat! God forbid!'

'We'll rest here until the evening,' said Jabbour, engrossed in
opening the tins of sardines, 'then we'll continue our journey by
night. It's better both for us and the car.'

He broke the loaf with his hands, then opened the bottle and
poured out two glasses.

'Let's agree as from now,' he said, handing him the glass – 'you
have two to my one. Don't forget I'm driving – also I'm not a
drinker like you.'

'And who told you I was a drinker?'

'You're a man of the city, besides I don't believe your life in
Europe was devoid of such things. As for me, I'm still a student,
and were my father to find out he'd immediately take his gun to

84

me – this despite the fact that he used to imbibe *laqbi* in his time. Ah, how cruel were our fathers, killing a date palm in order to get drunk from its heart.'

'Ah, Europe . . .' said Misbah Said, as though talking to himself.

Jabbour took a sandwich and added in the same tone:

'Europe, it took me over. I was like you.'

'Leave talk of Europe till after the third glass,' Jabbour interrupted, handing him his second glass. 'It's a subject that greatly interests me. They promised to send me on a scholarship to France so as to further my career as an agricultural adviser. An agricultural adviser – what a job! Do you know how tedious it is? Ough, those Touareg refuse to participate in any agricultural project. They still believe themselves to be aristocrats, knights of the desert, and despise farming and farmers.'

He took a bite at the sandwich and mouthed the words as he chewed:

'But . . . they're good people . . . one must . . . help them.'

He turned towards Misbah Said who was leaning against the trunk of the tree and looking at the far horizon, a shimmering mirage.

'You seem to be worried. Don't think of Europe now. I told you, after the third glass. The third glass will make you reveal to me those secrets you don't want to reveal.'

'In Europe there aren't any secrets.'

'We shall see. We shall see. You seem to be worried despite the second glass. Ah, I've remembered – what's your opinion of the Governor of Ghat? It'll be a journalist's scoop. He's a modest man and didn't tell you how alone, with his three children, he was able to hold up a French unit of armoured cars in the aggression of 'fifty-seven. A fabulous man – don't forget this incident in your investigation.'

'I was like you,' Misbah interrupted him in a dreamy voice, 'before I went to Europe.'

He took the glass from Jabbour.

'Don't go to Europe,' he asserted firmly. 'I don't advise you . . .'

Jabbour raised his head enquiringly. Taking a cigarette from Jabbour, he added:

'It's difficult to explain.'

'Even after the third glass?'

'After even the tenth.'

For several minutes there was silence. Wiping the sweat that poured from his brow with the sleeve of his shirt, Jabbour said:

'I hope that you will take back with you some good copy about life in the south. I must say you're the first journalist to take his profession seriously in this country.'

Misbah Said watched the smoke from his cigarette floating in the air.

'Yeah,' he answered in a despairing tone, 'but I don't see any point in it all.'

Jabbour came and sat down beside him.

'Perhaps,' he said confidentially, embracing the vast emptiness with his gaze. 'But I don't see it like that. We are always capable of doing something for those unfortunate people. They are content with their misery, submitting to their misfortune as though it were God's destiny for them. Our task is to demolish in them this contentment, to make them believe that that evil lieutenant and his ally the Governor are no more than a couple of dummies who are appropriately employed sitting on chairs and writing suspect reports to the powers-that-be. It's difficult to demolish this contentment, but it's our duty to try.'

He drew on his cigarette and added:

'The press is one of the tools by which to bring it about.'

'The lieutenant's a good man.'

'Good?'

After a period of silence he added: 'Good people don't kill.'

'Kill?'

'Certainly. He killed and wounded sixty-four people in the demonstrations. Till now he hasn't forgiven me for having arranged those demonstrations. He tries to show affection for me but it's all a show – mere show and malice. He doesn't forget that they stripped him of two pips because of this crime, and he believes that I am still actively political among the people. As you see, one's personal interests are stronger than anything else.'

Astonishment showed in Misbah's eyes but he kept silent. He was looking at the mirage wrestling with the silence, the sands and the labyrinthine horizon.

The sun was beginning to set as the Land-Rover set off across the emptiness that stretched away endlessly.

'The desert – how dreary and frightening it is!' said Misbah as he looked out at it through the window.

Holding hard to the steering wheel, Jabbour commented:

'Yes, it's dreary and frightening, but it's like life, like existence itself, a secret that seems to be sunk in desolation and silence. It promises you everything, it promises you the most priceless thing that can be given to a traveller who has lost his way. It promises you water and when you look for the water all you find in front of you is a mirage – mirages and mirages, a sea of mirages. They dance in front of you and stick their tongue out at you in mockery, leading you on without purpose. But, mind, you must always resist. Don't give in to the mirage as being a mirage, for the desert mirage is nothing but an underlying enigma, behind which you must search for real water. Don't let despair take possession of you, for in the end, over there, behind that endless mirage, you will find a well, if not a complete oasis. The great thing is to resist – that's the first secret for dealing with the desert.'

He turned towards Misbah and asked him to light him a cigarette. After a period of silence broken only by the buzzing of the engine, he said:

'The desert's like a flirtatious woman. It is unassailable, coquettish, never giving itself from the first time. You must try to possess it, try to discover its secret so that you can make yourself master of it. You see no point in all that. I, though, I see the point in everything. It is this that the desert has taught me. As for Europe, it has taken you over because you submitted to it.'

Misbah made no comment whatsoever. He continued to watch the darkness flooding the emptiness, listening to the hum of the motor that bored into his ears and brought on his headache.

Jabbour stopped the car alongside a small sandy hillock. He got down, climbed the hillock and looked about him.

'It's the middle of the night,' he said, coming back down, 'and I don't see any sign of the lights of Oubari. It seems we've lost our way.'

Jumping down from the car, Misbah said in a tone of annoyance:

'We should have kept to the main road from the beginning.'

'Say rather that we shouldn't have got drunk – that's more to the point.' Jabbour laughed and threw himself down on the soft sands and took out the packet of cigarettes from his pocket.

'I wanted to take a short cut,' he said quietly, having lit the cigarette. 'I relied on my experience but it appears that the desert doesn't excuse those who are drunk. If you want us not to commit a fourth mistake, then we must remain here till dawn. There's not enough petrol left to allow us to roam around the desert aimlessly. We haven't got sufficient reserves of petrol. That's our third mistake and the worst mistake of all. Come along, my dear fellow, tonight you're going to find yourself obliged to talk to me about Europe, if only to wile away the long night.'

He laughed cheerfully but stopped as he noticed Misbah's annoyance. The latter had collapsed on the cold sands and was looking at the sand dunes submerged in dark silence.

'The moon will soon show her face,' said Jabbour, as though to reassure him, having realized the reason for his unease. 'You'll see how magical the desert looks at night by moonlight. You'll enjoy its magic as it bares itself to you like a European woman. It will reveal to you one of its many secrets, as numerous as the grains of sand.'

Misbah Said listened intently. It seemed to him that the beating of drums and the noise of music pierced his ears, coming from somewhere close by, very close, from just behind or from on top of the sand hillock. Again he listened carefully: the beating of drums was more violent, the reverberation of the music more clamorous. It was an African rhythm, African drums – violent, clamorous, frenzied and mournful.

Misbah Said was so agitated that he was frightened he would divulge to his companion what he was hearing.

He made up his mind to occupy himself with something so as to drive away the hallucination and began to sing an old folk song.

The moon with its pallid mien began to steal out from behind the sand hillock. Still in the grip of his agitation, Misbah enquired:

'Jabbour, don't you think there are tribes living near here? The Touareg, for instance?'

'The Touareg don't live in the open air,' Jabbour said as he stretched out lazily on the sand, smoking a cigarette. He crossed his legs and looked out into space. 'These wastes are inhabited only by wolves and silence and various reptiles. That's at night – as for daytime there's the sun and the mirages.'

'How strange! It seemed to me a short while ago . . .' He hesitated before making known his secret: 'I heard the beating of drums and music being played on some weird instrument.'

'You see,' commented Jabbour with a smile, 'this is the first of the secrets.'

'You're joking.'

'I'm not joking,' Jabbour broke in seriously. 'These are the drums of the desert.'

'Drums of the desert?' asked Misbah in a childish tone. 'You're making fun.'

'I'm not making fun. The desert's a living being, like man. It has a soul and a spirit and pores to its skin. It suffers. It dances at night, it sings, it beats drums, plays music. It cheers itself up, generally after the torment of an intensely hot day. You don't know the desert, Misbah.'

Misbah kept silent and Jabbour rose and turned towards the pallid moon.

'You don't know,' he added, 'the secret of the success of African music – it's because it's drawn forth from the bowels of this desert. They knew that looking at it would drive them to madness, so they participated with it in its dance and its joy and thus they conquered it by conquering their own fear of it. Had they maintained the attitude of the onlooker they would have been gripped by terror and madness. They deal with it as they deal with life. I confess that I was gripped by terror the first time I heard those drums, but after that I got used to them.'

'I've never heard about it before.'

'And you won't hear about it. You city-dwellers, you isolate yourselves in your cities and complain about life and other things, so how do you hope to understand the desert? I've told you, the desert's a woman whom it is difficult to know from the beginning. You need to be on intimate terms with her for a longer time if you are determined to discover her secret.'

He pulled off his sandals and plunged his hands and feet into the cold sands.

'How sad this desert is!' he said in a choked voice. 'It is tortured by day, its bones being crushed by the sun. It makes complaint of its eternal sadness by playing magical tunes on the tiny particles of sand. It plays and plays, beating the drums until morning overtakes it, when once again it throws its body into the arms of its executioner, the sun. And so the journey of eternal torment continues.'

Jabbour had his head lowered towards the ground, his hands and feet thrust into the cold sand. It seemed to Misbah Said that he would burst into tears. He went on regarding him in silence, then there penetrated to his ears the sounds of drumming – surging, sad and frenzied.

Before reaching the main road they were out of petrol. Jabbour jumped from the Land-Rover and took down with him the gallon of water.

'Having been in touch with the police post at al-Uwainat they'll come to our rescue. We must reach the main road by foot before they start their search.'

'Leaving the road was a mistake from the start.'

'The real mistake was getting drunk. I'm feeling thirsty already. I committed a sin the desert won't forgive me.'

He carried the water and they moved off in the direction of the main road.

It was midday. The sun had drawn close to the desert's body, its flames unleashed. The last drop of water had gone but they hadn't yet reached the main road.

Misbah sat on the scorching sands to recover his breath, while Jabbour wiped the sweat away with his fingers and stared out at the vastness that stretched before him.

'I'm not going anywhere,' said Misbah, trying to moisten the walls of his mouth and his dry lips with a parched tongue. 'I can't make it.'

Jabbour stretched out his arms to help him, but the latter firmly shook his head in a sign of refusal.

He heard him talking, then sitting down alongside him, then talking and talking and continuing to make gestures with his hands, but he no longer heard, was no longer listening, no longer seeing. Everything was immersed in darkness as Jabbour carried him on his shoulders. He would stagger and fall and then he'd drag him along by his feet, and the soft sands would frenziedly set up their sad, raucous music.

The sun's disk plunged down to embrace the horizon in an orange glow. The burning rays, ablaze like skewers, had beaten down the whole day on the township. With the lifting of the heat the reptiles and insects came out of their hiding-places to move around amongst the bushes, the areas of wasteland and the date palms. The people who had kept to their huts also came out and went to their cultivated fields and started up the pumps to fill the parched waterways.

In the courtyard in front of the guest-house a number of the inhabitants had gathered, with their large white turbans, to gaze curiously through the windows.

The Land-Rover arrived, raising behind it a long trail of dust. The inhabitants ran off to hide themselves among the date palms behind the municipality building. The lieutenant's tall form stepped out; he was dressed in uniform and two silver pips shone on his shoulders; in his right hand he carried a cane. He came to a stop in the courtyard of the guest-house and stood there for a while before entering.

'How do you feel now?' he asked without emotion, seating himself on a wooden chair.

Misbah Said sat up in the bed, leaning his back against the wall.

'Thanks be to God,' he said, 'I'm getting my strength back. What's the latest news?'

The lieutenant took out a packet of cigarettes and offered one to Misbah Said, who repeated his question as he lit a match for the lieutenant:

'What's the latest news?'

'Nothing new. I received the last call a short while ago – they haven't found anything yet. Cars are still out scouring the desert.'

The silence was pierced by the clamour of the crickets and the murmuring of the inhabitants who were again swarming round the house.

'You should ally yourself with them.'

'I'm afraid the time has passed,' the lieutenant replied to the suggestion. Outside the clamour of the crickets and the noise of the pumps grew louder in the silence. Then the lieutenant repeated:

'I'm afraid the time has passed.'

The hum of the pumps had grown silent, the inhabitants had taken themselves to their huts, and the night had become a stage for insects and reptiles and the silence broken by the persistent lament of the crickets. Seating himself cross-legged on the Persian carpet – he was dressed in civilian clothes – the lieutenant was preparing the green tea over a fire of hidden embers.

'They found him drowned in the well,' he said. 'He was totally naked.'

He denuded the coals of ashes with a fan made from palm fronds, and went on in a low voice:

'You know that thirst makes a man imagine that his clothes are so heavy on his body that he wants to free himself of everything. He does so as the moment draws near when man gets rid of his complex of being embarrassed to walk about naked.'

'Thirst,' he went on after a few moments of silence, 'thirst makes him forget that there's absolutely no point in arriving at the well without clothes. He would have been able to tear them up and make of them a rope which he could have let down into the well and sucked at the wet cloth. But he had freed himself of the clothes and thus faced a cruel choice: either to die of thirst above the well as he looked down at the water or to die of drowning in the water, that's to say in the well.'

He began stirring the tea. Without attempting to change his indifferent tone of voice, he continued:

'You can imagine what it means for a man to cover fifty kilometres only to die, far away over there, in the bottom of the well. He had resisted for a long time and had only thrown himself into it when he had lost all hope and was in a state of madness.'

He passed Misbah the tea in a small glass, which Misbah placed on the rug in front of him. He remained silent, his back in contact with the cold wall as he listened to the lament of the crickets outside. With his thumb he traced along the pattern adorning the Persian rug, then said quietly:

'You know, lieutenant, I heard a story about something that happened in al-Hammada al-Hamra at the time of the drought and famine. A bedouin met up with a robber under the open sky. The brigand wanted to rob him of his only camel, so the bedouin pleaded with him saying that it was the only one he possessed and promised to take him to a rich man of his acquaintance who was in need of someone to herd his camels and sheep. On the way to the rich man's village the robber trod on a mine that had been left over from the World War. When the robber felt the mine under his feet the emotion of human kindness was awakened within him and he told the bedouin to make good his escape. But the bedouin, amazed by the robber's humanity, insisted on digging a deep hole under the robber's feet. Having finished it, he told his companion to fall backwards into the hole just as soon as he had gone off to a sufficient distance. The bedouin went off until he was out of sight of the robber. The robber then withdrew his foot and fell into the ditch behind him. However, a stray piece of shrapnel struck the bedouin a mortal blow, while the robber escaped without a scratch. Do you understand me, lieutenant?'

'I understand you. I understand you.'

'It's always the innocent who die and the robbers who are left. Do you understand me, lieutenant?'

'I understand you. I understand you. Life . . . life – like the desert – knows no mercy. Life is a crime in the desert. I saw that written up in Tifinagb[1] on the walls of Mount Akakus and it was translated to me by a learned Sheikh from the Touareg.'

Misbah Said remained with his back in contact with the wall. After a few moments drumbeats burst forth from the bowels of the silence, a rhythm that was violent, raucous and frenzied, yet at the same time deeply sad.

The beats followed one another, and voices were raised in song: a strange singing that resembled wailing. He heard shouts and groans mixing with the singing and the clamour of the drums. He tried to drive the noise from his head. Despite himself he asked:

'Don't you hear the beating of drums?'

'Of course I hear it – it's the Touareg singing.'

'The Touareg?'

'The Touareg get together every week, on Fridays after midnight, to sing and dance to their drums until the morning. These are their customs.'

Then he rose and put on his shoes.

'You must rest. Tomorrow there's a long journey ahead of you.'

He closed the door behind him. After a while Misbah heard the sound of the Land-Rover's engine mingling with the beating of the drums. He listened for a few moments, then dressed and went out.

He threaded his way through the date palms immersed in darkness. He cut across the cemetery. Behind a sandy hillock he saw women garbed in black sitting in a circle round the drums and veiled men with large white turbans who were dancing, calling out to one another, and going into convulsions and striking their breasts with their fists.

He squatted down on top of the hillock and watched their frenzy and listened to their raucous drumming, their pained groans, their songs that were as sad as laments for the dead. The din pierced the darkness, the desert and the quietness of night.

The winds woke him early as they buffeted the glass of the windows and the doors. He sat waiting in the reception hall, with the dust embedding itself in his hair and round his neck and creeping in between his body and his clothes.

The lieutenant came in. He was wearing his summer uniform. Without greeting him he asked:

'Are you ready? We must set off before the storm gets worse so as to catch the afternoon plane. I've decided to take you along myself.'

The lieutenant sat behind the steering wheel and drove the Land-Rover at a dangerous speed for such a day when, with the dust, visibility was no more than three metres. A quarter of an hour passed without them exchanging a word, then the lieutenant asked:

'If you'd be kind enough, a cigarette.'

Misbah Said took the packet of cigarettes from his pocket and lit one for the lieutenant and one for himself. Drawing on his cigarette, the lieutenant said:

'One must enjoy everything.' Then he coughed and added: 'Even smoking.'

'Yes, one must enjoy everything,' commented Misbah mockingly. He affected a cough and added in imitation of the lieutenant's tone of voice: 'Even committing a crime.'

The lieutenant's lower lip trembled as he turned sharply to his companion.

'What?' he asked in surprise. 'What do you mean?'

'Nothing.'

He pressed down again on the accelerator as a silence rose up between them.

Misbah's face was flushed as he said with alarming calm:

'Why did you kill him?'

'I don't understand you.'

'You do. The people told me everything yesterday.'

After a moment of silence the lieutenant answered:

'The people! Perhaps they told you of some alleged enmity between him and me?'

'No, they told me of things other than the enmity.'

'I don't understand you.'

The silence had risen up between them like a mountain, but Misbah Said seized hold of the lieutenant's arm in a sudden convulsive movement as he shouted:

'You understand all right . . . you understand.'

The lieutenant had to break and bring the car to a complete

stop. Without his features expressing any anger or agitation he removed the hand that clutched at his arm.

The dust storm had worsened so much that it was impossible to see ahead at all. The lieutenant preferred to wait till the storm calmed down and brought the car to a stop at the side of the road. He took out a packet of cigarettes and offered one to Misbah, who refused with a shudder. The lieutenant lit his own cigarette and said quietly through the cloud of smoke:

'There are many things you don't know about, very many things.'

'But I know many things. It is enough for me as from today to know that a man of the law can commit a crime before the world and remain free.'

'Do you consider that a crime?'

'Yes, it was possible for you to have saved him.'

'A man of the law is not responsible for saving anyone.'

'But you are responsible, in fact you're under an obligation to do so.'

'Now we're getting close. Listen. Listen well. A man who chooses the life of the desert must not rely on anyone. Because he is not subservient to anyone's authority, he enjoys utter freedom, even if he doesn't know what to do with this freedom except to chase after gazelles or mirages. When he's thirsty or in difficulties he must rely on himself, he must pay the price of the complete freedom he enjoys because of his being free of authority.'

Misbah Said began to tremble. He drew close to the lieutenant as he said:

'Had Jabbour been free of authority he would not have depended on you.'

They exchanged a quick glance before the lieutenant said:

'Had he been subject to authority, why did he dare to raise his voice against me so as to win over those idiotic locals to his side? He knew that no one would come to his rescue for the Touareg had taught him to lead an ascetic life and choose the desert, and his death was the price for defending this freedom. This authority does not protect those who raise their voices in opposition to it. So long as the authority provides you with bread and takes upon itself to care for you and look after you and protect you, it will certainly break your head in if you try to show enmity. It makes payment to you in exchange for your keeping quiet, it buys your eternal silence, but if you've taken your freedom then all you can do is to have recourse to the desert.'

'Your justification is barbarous, uglier than the crime,' said Misbah in a threatening tone. 'But wait – you'll see when I arrive at the capital. I'll expose you in the papers. I'll write the details of the crime and I'll not rest till you're brought to trial.'

'You'll profit nothing from that,' said the lieutenant with a smile. 'You haven't a single piece of evidence with which to convict me. The real crime was committed by the desert. Nothing killed him but his aspiring to freedom. Freedom is the criminal which should be brought to trial. All I did was to be late, just a little late. I did that on purpose: several hours or perhaps half a day. The rest of the job the desert was able to do on my behalf. I had to do it – a small punishment in the name of authority against which he had rebelled, refusing to take the bread from its hand. As for my confessions, there is no witness except yourself and you require a third party to establish my crime, as you call it.'

'But there are the locals, they'll testify in my favour. They told me of your hatred and that of the Governor and provincial officers for him; they are sympathetic towards him and will testify against you. You hate him because he knows the truth about you and I'll expose . . .'

'That's enough of that,' the lieutenant interrupted him coldly. 'Knowledge of the truth in our time is a justification that is all too sufficient for being punished. Listen – my own brother was also in opposition.'

He was silent for a while as he watched the dust sweeping across the windscreen.

Then, his voice quavering, he went on:

'He was stubbornly in opposition at the beginning of independence and it wasn't long before the authorities recognized how dangerous he was. Then, all of a sudden, he disappeared.'

'Disappeared?' An exclamation of surprise escaped from Misbah Said's lips.

'Yes, he disappeared from that time until today.'

'Where would he have disappeared to?'

Ignoring his question, the lieutenant continued:

'That day I discovered the truth: I had to make a choice: either to keep to the truth or to ignore it for ever.'

'To betray your conscience?'

'Yes, I wanted to live. I chose to keep possession of my bread and butter.'

'You took bread in exchange for truth,' commented Misbah Said scornfully.

'And why not?'

'You betrayed your conscience.'

'And why not?'

Silence rose up between them like a wall. A little later the lieutenant looked out of the window, then turned to Misbah Said and in a tone which, for the first time, was devoid of any harshness, said:

'I trust you've understood me.'

He turned the switch and put his foot down on the accelerator.

In the cafeteria of Sebha Airport the two of them sat facing one another after Misbah had checked in his luggage. After a long silence he said:

'Thanks for everything.'

The lieutenant remained silent, his eyes roving among the passengers.

The loudspeaker system informed passengers that they should make their way to the plane, so Misbah rose to his feet, only to find that the lieutenant was already standing in front of him, his hand held out to him as though it were a revolver. Misbah shook the hand and they exchanged a quick glance.

Before Misbah disappeared amidst the crowd of other passengers the lieutenant had caught up with him and said in a hissed whisper:

'Don't count too much on the locals,' and bade him farewell with an enigmatic smile.

Note
1. The script of the Tareef.

NABIL GORGY

Cairo is a Small City

On the balcony of his luxury flat Engineer Adil Salim stood
watching some workmen putting up a new building across the
wide street along the centre of which was a spacious garden. The
building was at the foundations stage, only the concrete foundations and some of the first-floor columns having been
completed. A young ironworker with long hair was engaged on
bending iron rods of various dimensions. Adil noticed that the
young man had carefully leant his Jawa motorcycle against a
giant crane that crouched at rest awaiting its future tasks. 'How
the scene has changed!' Adil could still remember the picture of
old-time master craftsmen, and of the workers who used to carry
large bowls of mixed cement on their calloused shoulders.

The sun was about to set and the concrete columns of a number
of new constructions showed up as dark frameworks against the
light in this quiet district at the end of Heliopolis.

As on every day at this time there came down into the garden
dividing the street a flock of sheep and goats that grazed on its
grass, with behind them two bedouin women, one of whom rode
a donkey, while the younger one walked beside her. As was his
habit each day, Adil fixed his gaze on the woman walking in her
black gown that not so much hid as emphasized the attractions of
her body, her waist being tied round with a red band. It could be
seen that she wore green plastic slippers on her feet. He wished
that she would catch sight of him on the balcony of his luxurious
flat; even if she did so, Adil was thinking, those bedouin had a
special code of behaviour that differed greatly from what he was
used to and rendered it difficult to make contact with them.
What, then, was the reason, the motive, for wanting to think up
some way of talking to her? It was thus that he was thinking,

following her with his gaze as she occasionally chased after a lamb that was going to be run over by a car or a goat left far behind the flock.

Adil, who was experienced in attracting society women, was aware of his spirit being enthralled: days would pass with him on the balcony, sunset after sunset, as he watched her without her even knowing of his existence.

Had it not been for that day on which he had been buying some fruit and vegetables from one of the shopkeepers on Metro Street, and had not the shopkeeper seen another bedouin woman walking behind another flock, and had he not called out to her by name, and had she not come, and had he not thrown her a huge bundle of waste from the shop, after having flirted with her and fondled her body – had it not been for that day, Adil's mind would not have given birth to the plan he was determined, whatever the cost, to put through, because of that woman who had bewitched his heart.

As every man, according to Adil's philosophy of life, had within him a devil, it was sometimes better to follow this devil in order to placate him and avoid his tyranny. Therefore Engineer Adil Salim finally decided to embark upon the terrible, the unthinkable. He remembered from his personal history during the past forty years that such a temporary alliance with this devil of his had gained him a courage that had set him apart from the rest of his colleagues, and through it he had succeeded in attaining this social position that had enabled him to become the owner of this flat whose value had reached a figure which he avoided mentioning even in front of his family lest they might be upset or feel envy.

Thus, from his balcony on the second floor in Tirmidhi Street, Engineer Adil Salim called out in a loud voice 'Hey, girl!' as he summoned the one who was walking at the rear of the convoy. When the flock continued on its way without paying any attention, he shouted again: 'Hey, girl – you who sell sheep,' and before the girl moved far away he repeated the word 'sheep'. Adil paid no attention to the astonishment of the doorman, who had risen from the place where he had been sitting at the entrance, thinking that he was being called. In fact he quietly told him to run after the two bedouin women and to let them know that he had some bread left over which he wanted to give them for their sheep.

From the balcony Adil listened to the doorman calling to the two women in his authoritative Upper Egyptian accent, at which they came to a stop and the one who was riding the donkey looked back at him. Very quickly Adil was able to make out her face as she looked towards him, seeking to discover what the matter was. As for the young girl, she continued on behind the flock. The woman was no longer young and had a corpulent body and a commanding look which she did not seek to hide from him. Turning her donkey round, she crossed the street separating the garden from his building and waited in front of the gate for some new development. Adil collected up all the bread in the house and hurried down with it on a brass tray. Having descended to the street, he went straight up to the woman and looked at her. When she opened a saddlebag close by her leg, he emptied all the bread into it.

'Thanks,' said the woman as she made off without turning towards him. He, though, raising his voice so that she would hear, called out, 'And tomorrow too.'

During a period that extended to a month Adil began to buy bread which he did not eat. Even on those days when he had to travel away or to spend the whole day far from the house, he would leave a large paper parcel with the doorman for him to give to the bedouin woman who rode the donkey and behind whom walked she for whom the engineer's heart craved.

Because Adil had a special sense of the expected and the probable, and after the passing of one lunar month, and in his place in front of the building, with the bread on the brass tray, there occurred that which he had been wishing would happen, for the woman riding the donkey had continued on her way and he saw the other, looking around her carefully before crossing the road, ahead of him, walking towards him. She was the most beautiful thing he had set eyes on. The speed of his pulse almost brought his heart to a stop. How was it that such beauty was to be found without it feeling embarrassed at ugliness, for after it any and every thing must needs be so described? When she was directly in front of him, and her kohl-painted eyes were scrutinizing him, he sensed a danger which he attributed to her age, which was no more than twenty. How was it that she was so tall, her waist so slim, her breasts so full, and how was it that her buttocks swayed so enticingly as she turned away and went off with the bread, having thanked him? His imagination became frozen even though she was still close to him: her pretty face with the high cheekbones, the fine nose and delicate lips, the silver, crescent-shaped earrings, and the necklace that graced her bosom? Because such beauty was 'beyond the permissible', Adil went on thinking about Salma – for he had got to know her name, her mother having called her by it in order to hurry her back lest the meeting between the lovers be prolonged.

Adil no longer troubled about the whistles of the workers who had now risen floor by floor in the building opposite him, being in a state of infatuation, his heart captured by this moonlike creature. After the affair, in relation to himself, having been one of boldness, to end in seeing or greeting her, it now became a matter of necessity that she turn up before sunset at the house so that he might not be deprived of the chance of seeing her. So it was that Engineer Adil Salim fell in love with the beautiful bedouin girl Salma. And just as history is written by historians, so it was that Adil and his engineering work determined the history of this passion in the form of a building each of whose columns represented a day and each of whose floors was a month. He noted that, at the completion of twenty-eight days and exactly at full moon, Salma would come to him in place of her mother to take the bread. And so, being a structural engineer, he began to observe the moon, his yearning increasing when it was in eclipse and his spirits sparkling as its fullness drew near till, at full moon, the happiness of the lover was completed by seeing the beloved's face.

During seven months he saw her seven times, each time seeing in her the same look she had given him the first time: his heart would melt, all resolution would be squeezed out of him and that fear for which he knew no reason would be awakened. She alone was now capable of granting him his antidote. After the seventh month Salma, without any preamble, had talked to him at length, informing him that she lived with her parents around a spring at a distance of an hour's walk to the north of the airport, and that it consisted of a brackish spring alongside which was a sweet one, so that she would bathe in the first and rinse herself clean in the other, and that there were date palms around the two springs, also grass and pasturage. Her father, the owner of the springs and the land around them, had decided to invite him and so tomorrow 'he'll pass by you and invite you to our place, for tomorrow we attend to the shearing of the sheep'.

Adil gave the lie to what he was hearing, for it was more than any stretch of the imagination could conceive might happen.

The following day Adil arrived at a number of beautifully made tents where a vast area of sand was spread out below date palms that stretched to the edge of a spring. Around the spring was gathered a large herd of camels, sheep and goats that spoke of the great wealth of the father. It was difficult to believe that such a place existed so close to the city of Cairo. If Adil's astonishment was great when Salma's father passed by him driving a new Peugeot, he was yet further amazed at the beauty of the area surrounding this spring. 'It's the land of the future,' thought Adil to himself. If he were able to buy a few *feddans* now he'd become a millionaire in a flash, for this was the Cairo of the future. 'This is the deal of a lifetime,' he told himself.

On the way the father asked a lot of questions about Adil's work and where he had previously lived and about his knowledge of the desert and its people. Though Adil noticed in the father's tone something more than curiosity, he attributed this to the nature of the bedouin and their traditions.

As the car approached the tents Adil noticed that a number of men were gathered under a tent whose sides were open, and as the father and his guest got out of the car the men turned round, seated in the form of a horse-shoe. With the father sitting down and seating Engineer Adil Salim alongside him, one of the sides of the horse-shoe was completed. In front of them sat three men on whose faces could be seen the marks of time in the form of interlaced wrinkles.

The situation so held Adil's attention that he was unaware of Salma except when she passed from one tent to another in the direction he was looking and he caught sight of her gazing towards him.

The man who was sitting in a squatting position among the three others spoke. Adil heard him talking about the desert, water and sheep, about the roads that went between the oases and the *wadi*, the towns and the springs of water, about the bedouin tribes and blood ties; he heard him talking about the importance of protecting these roads and springs, and the palm trees and the dates, the goats and the milk upon which the suckling child would be fed; he also heard him talk about how small the *wadi* was in comparison to this desert that stretched out endlessly.

In the same way as Adil had previously built the seven-storey building that represented the seven months, each month containing twenty-eight days, till he would see Salma's face whenever it was full moon, he likewise sensed that this was the tribunal which had been set up to make an enquiry with him into the killing of the man whom he had one day come across on the tracks between the oases of Kharga and Farshout. It had been shortly after sunset when he and a friend, having visited the iron ore mines in the oases of Kharga had, instead of taking the asphalt road to Assiout, proceeded along a rough track that took them down towards Farshout near to Kena, as his friend had to make a report about the possibility of repairing the road and of extending the railway line to the oases. Going down from the high land towards the *wadi*, the land at a distance showing up green, two armed men had appeared before them. Adil remembered how, in a spasm of fear and astonishment, of belief and disbelief, and with a speed that at the time he thought was imposed upon him, a shot had been fired as he pressed his finger on the trigger of the revolver which he was using for the first time. A man had fallen to the ground in front of him and, as happens in films, the other had fled. As for him and his friend, they had rushed off to their car in order to put an end to the memory of the incident by reaching the *wadi*. It was perhaps because Adil had once killed a man that he had found the courage to accept Salma's father's invitation.

'That day,' Adil heard the man address him, 'with a friend in a car, you killed Mubarak bin Rabia when he went out to you, Ziyad al-Mihrab being with him.'

This was the manner in which Engineer Adil Salim was executed in the desert north-west of the city of Cairo: one of the men held back his head across a marble-like piece of stone, then another man plunged the point of a tapered dagger into the spot that lies at the bottom of the neck between the two bones of the clavicle.

HANAN SHAYKH

The Persian Carpet

When Maryam had finished plaiting my hair into two pigtails, she put her finger to her mouth and licked it, then passed it over my eyebrows, moaning: 'Ah, what eyebrows you have – they're all over the place!' She turned quickly to my sister and said: 'Go and see if your father's still praying.' Before I knew it my sister had returned and was whispering 'He's still at it,' and she stretched out her hands and raised them skywards in imitation of him. I didn't laugh as usual, nor did Maryam; instead, she took up the scarf from the chair, put it over her hair and tied it hurriedly at the neck. Then, opening the wardrobe carefully, she took out her handbag, placed it under her arm and stretched out her hands to us. I grasped one and my sister the other. We understood that we should, like her, proceed on tiptoe, holding our breath as we made our way out through the open front door. As we went down the steps, we turned back towards the door, then towards the window. Reaching the last step, we began to run, only stopping when the lane had disappeared out of sight and we had crossed the road and Maryam had stopped a taxi.

Our behaviour was induced by fear, for today we would be seeing my mother for the first time since her separation by divorce from my father. He had sworn he would not let her see us, for, only hours after the divorce, the news had spread that she was going to marry a man she had been in love with before her family had forced her into marrying my father.

My heart was pounding. This was not from fear or from running but was due to anxiety and a feeling of embarrassment about the meeting that lay ahead. Though in control of myself and my shyness, I knew that I would be incapable – however much I tried – of showing my emotions, even to my mother; I would be unable to throw myself into her arms and smother her with kisses and clasp her head as my sister would do with such spontaneity. I had thought long and hard about this ever since Maryam had whispered in my ear – and in my sister's – that my mother had come from the south and that we were to visit her secretly the following day. I began to imagine that I would make myself act exactly as my sister did, that I would stand behind her and imitate her blindly. Yet I know myself: I have committed myself to myself by heart. However much I tried to force myself, however much I thought in advance about what I should and shouldn't do, once I was actually faced by the situation and was standing looking down at the floor, my forehead puckered into an even deeper frown, I would find I had forgotten what I had resolved to do. Even then, though, I would not give up hope but would implore my mouth to break into a smile; it would none the less be to no avail.

When the taxi came to a stop at the entrance to a house, where two lions stood on columns of red sandstone, I was filled with delight and immediately forgot my apprehension. I was over-come with happiness at the thought that my mother was living in a house where two lions stood at the entrance. I heard my sister imitate the roar of a lion and I turned to her in envy. I saw her stretching up her hands in an attempt to clutch the lions. I thought to myself: She's always uncomplicated and jolly, her gaiety never leaves her, even at the most critical moments – and here she was, not a bit worried about this meeting.

But when my mother opened the door and I saw her, I found myself unable to wait and rushed forward in front of my sister and threw myself into her arms. I had closed my eyes and all the joints of my body had grown numb after having been unable to be at rest for so long. I took in the unchanged smell of her hair, and I discovered for the first time how much I had missed her and wished that she would come back and live with us, despite the tender care shown to us by my father and Maryam. I couldn't rid my mind of that smile of hers when my father agreed to divorce her, after the religious sheikh had intervened following her threats to pour kerosene over her body and set fire to herself if my father wouldn't divorce her. All my senses were numbed by that smell of her, so well preserved in my memory. I realized how much I had missed her, despite the fact that after she'd hurried off behind her brother to get into the car, having kissed us and started to cry, we had continued with the games we were playing in the lane outside our house. As night came, and for the first time in a long while we did not hear her squabbling with my father, peace and quiet descended upon the house – except that is for the weeping of Maryam, who was related to my father and had been living with us in the house ever since I was born.

Smiling, my mother moved me away from her so that she could hug and kiss my sister, and hug Maryam again, who had begun to cry. I heard my mother, who was in tears, say to her 'Thank you', and she wiped her tears with her sleeve and looked me and my sister up and down, saying: 'God keep them safe, how they've sprung up!' She put both arms round me, while my sister buried her head in my mother's waist, and we all began to laugh when we found that it was difficult for us to walk like that. Reaching the inner room, I was convinced her new husband was inside because my mother said, smiling: 'Mahmoud loves you very much and he would like it if your father would give you to me so that you can live with us and become his children too.' My sister laughed and answered: 'Like that we'd have two fathers.' I was still in a benumbed state, my hand placed over my mother's arm, proud at the way I was behaving, at having been able without any effort to be liberated from myself, from my shackled hands, from the prison of my shyness, as I recalled to mind the picture of my meeting with my mother, how I had spontaneously thrown myself at her, something I had thought wholly impossible, and my kissing her so hard I had closed my eyes.

Her husband was not there. As I stared down at the floor I froze. In confusion I looked at the Persian carpet spread on the floor, then gave my mother a long look. Not understanding the significance of my look, she turned and opened a cupboard from which she threw me an embroidered blouse, and moving across to a drawer in the dressing-table, she took out an ivory comb with red hearts painted on it and gave it to my sister. I stared down at the Persian carpet, trembling with burning rage. Again I looked at my mother and she interpreted my gaze as being one of tender longing, so she put her arms round me, saying: 'You must come every other day, you must spend the whole of Friday at my place.' I remained motionless, wishing that I could remove her arms from around me and sink my teeth into that white forearm. I wished that the moment of meeting could be undone and re-enacted, that she could again open the door and I could stand there – as I should have done – with my eyes staring down at the floor and my forehead in a frown.

The lines and colours of the Persian carpet were imprinted on my memory. I used to lie on it as I did my lessons; I'd be so close to it that I'd gaze at its pattern and find it looking like slices of red water-melon repeated over and over again. But when I sat down on the couch, I would see that each slice of melon had changed into a comb with thin teeth. The clusters of flowers surrounding its four sides were purple-coloured. At the beginning of summer my mother would put mothballs on it and on the other ordinary carpets and would roll them up and place them on top of the cupboard. The room would look stark and depressing until autumn came, when she would take them up to the roof and spread them out. She would gather up the mothballs, most of which had dissolved from the summer's heat and humidity, then, having brushed them with a small broom, she'd leave them there. In the evening she'd bring them down and lay them out where they belonged. I would be filled with happiness as their bright colours once again brought the room back to life. This particular carpet, though, had disappeared several months before my mother was divorced. It had been spread out on the roof in the sun and in the afternoon my mother had gone up to get it and hadn't found it. She had called my father and for the first time I had seen his face flushed with anger. When they came down from the roof, my mother was in a state of fury and bewilderment. She got in touch with the neighbours, all of whom swore they hadn't seen it. Suddenly my mother exclaimed: 'Ilya!' Everyone stood speechless: not a word from my father or from my sister or from our neighbours Umm Fouad and Abu Salman. I found myself crying out: 'Ilya? Don't say such a thing, it's not possible.'

Ilya was an almost blind man who used to go round the houses of the quarter repairing cane chairs. When it came to our turn, I would see him, on my arrival back from school, seated on the stone bench outside the house with piles of straw in front of him and his red hair glinting in the sunlight. He would deftly take up the strands of straw and, like fishes, they'd slip through the mesh. I would watch him as he coiled them round with great dexterity, then bring them out again until he had formed a circle of straw for the seat of the chair, just like the one that had been there before. Everything was so even and precise: it was as though his hands were a machine and I would be amazed at the speed and nimbleness of his fingers. Sitting as he did with his head lowered, it looked as though he were using his eyes. I once doubted that he could see more than vague shapes in front of him, so I squatted down and looked into his rosy-red face and was able to see his half-closed eyes behind his glasses. They had in them a white line that pricked at my heart and sent me hurrying off to the kitchen, where I found a bag of dates on the table, and I heaped some on a plate and gave them to Ilya.

I continued to stare at the carpet as the picture of Ilya, red of face and hair, appeared to me. I was made aware of his hand as he walked up the stairs on his own; of him sitting on his chair, of his bargaining over the price for his work, of how he ate and knew that he had finished everything on the plate, of his drinking from the pitcher, with the water flowing easily down his throat. Once at midday, having been taught by my father that before entering a Muslim house he should say 'Allah' before knocking at the door and entering, as a warning to my mother in case she were unveiled, my mother rushed at him and asked him about the carpet. He made no reply, merely making a sort of sobbing noise. As he walked off, he almost bumped into the table and, for the first time, tripped. I went up to him and took him by the hand. He knew me by the touch of my hand, because he said to me in a half-whisper: 'Never mind, child.' Then he turned round to leave. As he bent over to put on his shoes, I thought I saw tears on his cheeks. My father didn't let him leave before saying to him: 'Ilya, God will forgive you if you tell the truth.' But Ilya walked off, steadying himself against the railings. He took an unusually long time as he felt his way down the stairs. Then he disappeared from sight and we never saw him again.

ABDUL ILAH ABDUL RAZZAK

Voices from Near and Far

Squatting down on the ground, he took out a rectangular pad with a torn cover from a low shelf alongside him. He then rummaged in his pockets and produced a pale-coloured pencil. Without waiting for her to say anything he pressed the tip of the pencil against the top of the piece of paper and began to write slowly. Certain slight signs of concentration marked his narrow forehead that jutted out from the fold of his head-dress. Then she saw him turning his face towards her with a sort of enquiring movement.

'Is there anything else?'

'What have you written?'

His head moved in a semblance of irritation. Without looking at the paper he said:

'A long time has passed and I haven't . . .'

'Three months.'

He wasn't there and there was no news of him. She found herself facing a real fear that continued to spread through her furiously, a fear that would not come to terms with her, would not give way to the boldness of hope.

Again he moved the pen, adding:

'No letter's come to you from him. I've said to him: "Write as soon as you get this letter," also that you're disturbed about him and that you're always wondering how he is.'

She raised her hand in front of her as though wishing to say something, but then she froze. Lowering her head, she said slowly:

'Tell him I'm worried.'

Lifting up a torn shred from the remains of the cover of the pad that jogged about in his hands, he answered:

'I've written that.'

Wringing her hands nervously, she said:

'Write: A letter arrived from Isma'il to his family, while I, while I . . .'

She swallowed her spittle.

At the time, before the incident had upset her, they said to her that Isma'il sent her son's greetings to her and that like him he was well . . . Why hadn't he done like Isma'il? . . . We're telling you? We're far away, very far away and two letters posted in the same box, it wouldn't be long before they got separated. The smallest mistake was liable to make one of them go astray and it could make its way here or go off somewhere else. A long time might go by till it found its way to you. Just be patient a little.

He looked into her face, moved the pencil over the paper slowly, then stopped a while to think and continued writing rather fast. Again he raised his head:

'Anything else?'

She was silent. She stared up at the ceiling which was open to the empty space ablaze with the sun's rays. Before she closed her eyelids a small, scattered flock of birds moved across the narrow space coming from the direction of the distant marshes. She rubbed at her nose, then shook her head as she said with a sigh:

'Can he come back on leave? Others do . . . Write . . .'

The man continued to write. She bent over slightly and said:

'And write to him also that I . . . that I no longer believe . . .'

It was on just such a day. He was looking into her eyes and the suitcase was swaying in his hand and the door giving out on to the sun. When he turned away from her to leave he lingered for a while. Certainly something was troubling him at the time. Certainly he had heard something . . . She herself was not in a mood that allowed her to be in a state of such complete awareness that she could observe both herself and him. When he had arrived closer to the door she had stretched out her hand automatically and had said nothing. He, though, acting like someone who had anticipated such a movement from her, had inclined his head to one side in an attempt to turn around. However, he came to a stop in the empty doorway where his figure was blocking the sun's light and there was a dark patch touching his shoulders. When she had looked long at him her eyes clouded over because of the mingling of light with the shadows, and when she opened them again the door was slowly closing on him and a high-pitched whistling was reverberating in her ears in a way that hurt her.

He darted an enquiring glance at her:

'What do you mean?'

She coughed hard, then added in a tense tone:

'No. It's not that, it's just . . . tell him I'm frightened.'

It was real fear. The fear brought about by inner apprehensions never misses. Even the simple and good things are changed by it into an arid sadness. Prayers and hopes and striving, all are impotent in the face of inner apprehensions.

Turning the paper over, he said:

'I've said something similar to that. What more?'

She rested her hand on her bosom and said:

'It doesn't matter – write it again. Write it.'

Then, nervously, she pulled at her apron.

Coming back to the sheet of paper without interest, he added:

'And you are of course in good health?'

'Me?' she answered immediately.

He regarded her with concentration, in semi-astonishment. Moving his head back and forth, he said, as though talking to himself:

'Such things must be written.'

She gave a slight shudder, and as though she had recollected something, said quickly:

'Because of you I bought a radio and every night I listen to the soldiers' voices. Why don't you do the same as them? When will your turn come?'

Every night a furious joy would enwrap her, a feeling of joy that something must come about, something that is interwoven in the soldiers' voices and that shines despite the gloom of fear. The thing that occurs leaves within the area of itself some sort of an ending which may be now or tomorrow or the day after that, or during the days that are yet to come, so long as he exists and he continues to be. Therefore his voice will come with theirs, for nothing is stopping its continuance.

These voices, though, when she heard them, appeared the same because of the speed with which they talked. This required her to listen ever so carefully to every name that was given out, for it seemed to her that, if she were to be inattentive when listening to the names, the voices would scatter and coagulate, become like the voice of a single man, at times disjointed, at others flowing on, and between the flowing and the disjointedness was created this conformity or this strange similarity between them. More than once she asked herself: What is it that gives their voices this similar tone? Is it the love that binds them together? Or is it that great shared thing that unites them?

They are pleasant moments when they talk. Why, then, are they so frugal with their words? Is it the sensation of love for all the beautiful things that causes them to unite into a single voice, a single tone?

His hand wrote quickly then came to a stop. He stared at her with a blank gaze. She whispered to herself: I love them . . . those are my sons.

'What is it?'

But why do their voices seem so quick despite their strength, as though, like them, they were travelling as far away from being identified as they are far away from their families. Names that are of a kind and names that are dissimilar. Despite everything they unite in the intoxication of that one voice that proceeds from across remote distances.

He looked at her in astonishment. She averted her face slightly, then again whispered to herself:

'I think I forgot.'

'What?'

As she looked at him she gave a slight sigh, then said:

'I forgot to turn it off.'

She made a small gesture with her hand and a sort of smile came to her lips.

The palm of her hand climbed up the cold frame of the transistor radio and the voice of a soldier was held back in her hand.

'Not that one either,' she whispered, shaking her head.

A song comes to her from afar; it seems as though it is emanating from outside, from across the lonely waters in the thickets of reeds sleeping in the silent depths. The transistor radio was over there, broadcasting softly, its front turned aside.

Stretching his leg a little, the man said:

'I don't think there's anything else.'

She made not a sound. Her eyes were closed as she breathed in the freshness of a light breeze that stroked her gaunt forehead; she couldn't help but give herself up to it.

She heard the sound of the sheet of paper being torn from the pad.

When she looked up she saw that it alone was in his hands and that the pad was resting under a corner of the mat.

'Now read it out to me,' she said in a quavering voice as she drew slightly closer to him.

EDWARD EL-KHARRAT

Birds' Footsteps in the Sand

The world was in its first dawn, devoid of anyone. The virgin air, cloudless and of the desert, had at one and the same time the sea's moisture and a particular dryness.

The time was noon, quiet and utterly still.

The silence was not a solid one; it was a soft silence. Everything was soft and limpid.

I had returned to this world that never comes to an end, and yet I am a stranger in it; I know that I am not there.

My mother takes me by the hand as we get down from the train at the station in Abu Kir. We are alone: no one but us on the train or at the station.

The platforms are raised, standing directly on the clean yellow sand, their surfaces black, the paving stones glistening.

The station structure with its cool shaded entrance open to the sands on the other side, its triangular roof covered in red tiles, the solitary ticket office with its writing in Arabic and English, and the face of the stationmaster, motionless in the half-darkness behind the iron bars, looked like some enchanted building.

The great black hose, hanging down by its ribbed iron nozzle from the tank, is firmly muscled; its outer skin is damp and hot, with a cohesive stream of water spouting from it, striking the platform, then falling abruptly as though it were something solid, writhing and hunching itself and giving out a foam that is translucent, thick and white and that descends into the rectangular space between the two high platforms and runs along the wooden sleepers, between the iron rails that stretch out confidently to the evil-shaped iron buffers.

The driver got down from the strong, round-bellied locomotive, wholly black except for the gold-coloured writing on it, which was still spitting out thick gusts of white steam into the noon light. He bent down with his whole body and turned, with effort, a great horizontal wheel on the large tap that stood on the platform, at which the flow of water was cut off and changed into a thin trickle that came on and then stopped, dripping from the two sides of the platform on to the coarse sands that lay under the gravel, pebbles and coal dust and quickly and thirstily drank it up.

The man was silent as he worked; the water was silent, the station silent. There was no sound, no one.

I saw a solitary cart beside the station. The horse, clad in a broad brass collar that sparkled in the light, was alone, abandoned, thrusting its head deeply into the sack of straw, and suddenly the little brass bells that hung round its neck gave out a tinkling sound, their echoes quivering in the vast quietness, sharp and high-pitched, tiny and consecutive.

Escaping from my mother's hand, I set off at a run, with difficulty extracting my feet from the damp sand into which my shoes sank, the canvas shoes that I had cleaned very early that morning with blanco and a piece of flannel dipped into a coffee saucer full of water.

'In the name of the cross and the sign of the cross,' exclaimed my mother, but she didn't call me to her. She let me run off and I entered, on my own, into the broad, desert passageways between the huts and the cabins and the few one-storey stone houses, from behind their fences that were made of reeds implanted in the sand and tied together with rough, faded twine. As I ran with difficulty along the sands, I would touch them with my hand and the fencing would sway slightly. There were thin openings lengthwise between the reed supports that were scorchingly hot from the sun. The pathways rose and fell, all sandy and clean; the air rose in little eddies of fine sand, making a rustling noise in the brittle reed canes.

The decorations, perforated in geometrical and ornamental patterns in the wood of the closed cabins and the empty, sloping balconies whose paintwork was peeling, faced the light of noon with a special intimate darkness from within.

Between the cabins were random, irregular gaps, small and

narrow and ever shady, and on the sand were thin dry sheets of newspaper covered with grains of sand. The tops of lemonade bottles, rusty tins, and sharp dry bits of refuse were submerged in the sand; and rising out of it, between the cabin walls, were tilted date palms, their bark firm and ribbed, with the wind soughing in their tops that swayed with gracefully tremulous fronds.

From behind the huts I heard the dull, lilting call in the vast empty space: Kerosene . . . kerosene; the call had an echo that was full of a warning and a nostalgic desire that had no explanation.

Suddenly the kerosene cart appeared before me, very close, at the broad intersection, with its small, cylindrical body coloured red, on it the drawing of an open half of a shell and the writing extending along its belly, being pulled by a solitary slow bay horse, its head lowered, its eyes blinkered. The cart had large round wheels reaching up to its swollen middle, slowly turning and leaving in their wake two lines that bit deeply into the sand as it moved along on its way, encountering no one, no one responding to its call.

I told myself that we must be in early summer, very early in summer, perhaps just after Easter.

Our going to Sheikh Makar's cabin at Abu Kir was, on each occasion, a recurrent festive event about which there was no guarantee that it would come round again. There was, first of all, the exciting train journey, after which we would spend the whole day on the beach and in the cabin. While I would remain on the shore, my mother would go out to the last of the barrels in the sea, and beyond them, till I could see no more of her than a black dot. She would be wearing a swimsuit with long legs that showed no more of her than her two arms and was rounded at the throat. She would go down into the sea with her friend whom she called 'my darling Victoria', the daughter of the Protestant minister from Upper Egypt, with the square face and the eyes that were both tender and sly.

Tall and thin, Victoria's face was smooth and elongated and ended in a chin that appeared as sculpted, pointed and delicate; her eyes, tapering to the sides of her face, possessed a very calm and silent look; her voice was always soft, even her laugh was low and had a steady, even rhythm to it. With the short black swimming trunks stretched tight across my thighs, I put on the old white silk shirt which I wore when we went to the sea. I could hear her laugh from behind the wood of the adjoining room as she, together with my mother, took off her clothes.

I loved Victoria and would flee from her in shyness. I never wearied of gazing at her and I yearn deeply for her.

Upon this face has been deposited layers of love whose stormy waves bore forward time and time again and then drew back. I look at her with the clear love of a young man, in which, nevertheless, I am aware of all life's cracks and flaws.

Did my mother want to go alone and leave me with my sisters in the crowded house in Gheit al-Enab? And had I cried that day with those burning tears of disappointment that fall as the world itself falls? Had I forgotten this recurring drama which was so cruel for that child who has never grown up? Had I forgotten it as soon as the events had gone full circle? Had I run off to drag out my canvas shoes from amidst the jumble of things under the bed and to clean them with a coating of the blanco in the middle of which had been hollowed out a hole made smooth by the rag soaked in water? And had I put on my short black velvet trousers that I wore at celebrations and on feast days?

The floor of the shaded wooden corridor of the upper storey of the hut would shake under my feet and sway slightly, between the railing of the balcony that looked down on the street on the one side and the doors of the closed rooms on the other. The long thin cracks between the wooden floorboards would fascinate me: hot lines of noonday light below which, if I bent over and put my eyes to them, I could see the sand of the road.

When I went into the bathroom I was at a loss as to how the water came to the tap and the porcelain basin fixed to the wooden wall, and as to where the flush water went, suddenly gushing forth, then stopping and then once again bursting out, surging and of variable colour.

I descended the fragile, steep, dark-coloured steps, feeling their cool wood against the soles of my bare feet, and when I looked up I saw Victoria wrapping round her waist the belt of the soft, fluffy blue bathrobe, with slippers of a very old dark brown leather on her feet, and with her thin brown thighs rising up under the clinging robe and ending in the mysterious, magical darkness. Her breasts in the dark blue swimsuit with the high neck, faded by sun and water, were small, cone-shaped and delicate; they showed directly under the cloth of the swimsuit that clung to them and gently enfolded them, with nothing in between, so that the nipples took shape, rounded and protruding. She descended towards me slowly, as though not heeding. I saw her eyes smiling. We went down, racing each other. We were side by side on the narrow staircase, running.

She said to me: 'I've beaten you – first there eats the pear.'

She gave her mysterious laugh that was slightly husky. I lowered my face as the blood rushed to it in embarrassment and ran to the sands and was stung by their heat.

Had we gone down to the sea, and returned and eaten, and was I now alone in the afternoon in the utter silence, in the shady, humid gap between the sand of the road and the floor of the cabin, turning my hand around in the sand and feeling its dampness under the granular surface and thinking about the elongated body that the waters had taken far away from me, while I was on the sea shore in the middle of a small bay filled with translucent waters of a crystalline clarity in which wavy lines, as though drawn by a fine moving pen, fluttered, coming and going gently between the small glistening rocks which quickly dried and were again wetted?

How quickly the faded blue swimsuit was changed into a far-away dot in the vast sea! My mother had outstripped her to beyond the barrels, and I could hardly see her amidst the slight spray raised by the waves.

I was standing in the clear, shallow water and looking at the wooden bridge extending into the sea on short, circular columns of slimy cement on which quivered diaphanous green seaweed, sporting in the water and trembling like living creatures, then emerging wet from the surface of the water, the fibres intermingled, then suddenly drying and growing yellow, crisp and motionless as old paper.

Now, at noon, there was no one standing on the bridge with cane rods and pails of shrimps and small worms. The bridge, with its dry wood, stretched out far into the sea, unending.

The desolation on the shore was absolute. There was not a single bather on that calm noonday. The sunshades, scattered far apart and of ageing colours, threw their shade on to the empty, opened-out deck chairs; even the lifeguard, with his shrill whistle, was not there.

I was alone, not knowing how to enter the vast, frightening, deep, magical sea, not knowing how to turn back from it.

On the surface of the white sands were the untouched tracks of birds, small and clearly defined, following one another in a single curving line, then suddenly coming to an end.

I bowed my head slightly so as not to bump against the cabin floor and went in between the short, square, grey stone pillars. I had to bend down and crawl along the sand on my bare hands and knees. Old yellow pages of newspaper, buried in the sand, were rustled by a secret wind that came in a hot blast from the sun outside. The garbage can at the corner of the cabin in the narrow passageway gave out a dry, slightly putrid smell, unfamiliar and not disquieting. I could feel the movement of the floor above me as it shook slightly under footsteps, and I would be excited by a clear picture of delicate thighs stripped of clothing and moving about naked in a closed room with wooden walls, radiant with light stealing in from behind the cracked wood of the boards.

As my hands rummaged in the sand they came across a small blue bottle with a rounded body, embossed with tiny letters I couldn't make out. I knew it was a bottle of perfume like those I would find at home on the marble slab of the dressing-table in front of the mirror alongside the silver kohl container with the thin stick at the mere sight of which my eyelids would quiver, and a brass box of powder with its small mirror, and yellow hairpins with two tightly contiguous prongs.

The bottle was filled with sand which I emptied out, cleaning it carefully yet impatiently with my hands. Then I crawled out quickly, my head lowered and my knees scraping against the moist sand.

I went up the steps at a run and rushed into the living-room where my mother was stretched out on the ottoman with the coloured cushions. I came to an abrupt stop when I saw Victoria sitting at the end of the couch, alongside my mother's feet, her back resting against a soft pillow, her arms raised as she combed her hair with rhythmic movements, gentle and feminine; the look in her eyes was far-away and had in it neither sadness nor silence: it was as though she had left us all and didn't know where she was.

I rushed to my mother, saying: 'Look what I've found.' I stretched out my hand to her with the magical blue bottle that now shone with the sweat of my hands that had been grasping it like some treasure. My mother smiled and said without anger: 'What things the crow brings to its mother!' She didn't take the bottle from me and I didn't cry.

I walked by the edge of the water on the sea shore, with the world deserted, inside my body a pleasing sense of exhaustion, the awakening blood of youth and a slight burning from the sea's sun. With the water not yet dried, I could see it gleaming on my skin, which glowed and pulsated in regular throbs of heat.

The limpid blue waters under my feet were shallow. They were almost motionless except for a slow ripple. They contained the expanse of the imprisoned, upturned sky, slightly deeper in its blueness than the vast emptiness lit up by the sun, an expanse that mingled with the bed of soft sand, smooth and sleek, on whose surface my feet scarcely left any tracks. Once again I extracted my legs from this under-sky and put my wet feet on the first of the marble steps, which swayed with a gentle trembling as though broken and rose suddenly from the skin of the translucent waters that could hardly be seen. The rich, white marble was as old and smooth as vintage wine. The edges of the steps that rose in a scarcely perceptible curve entered anew, in the direction of the sea, into a wide sweep as they ascended towards the scorching sky, step by step, towering and unhurried, with their smooth marble, delicate yet firm, the pores on the outer skin rendering it even smoother. It had been dried by the sun, and the little water left on it by my feet was evaporating, a coating that was soon dispersed and scarcely left any trace other than a dark patch in the tone of the marble, which became more sparkling. I would feel its heat under my feet as I climbed up further and as, little by little, the last drops of water wetting my feet dried away.

In my ascent of these endless stairs there was an eagerness, a lively expectancy; it was as though I would be finding something I didn't know about but which I yearned for deeply, something that excited me, over there in the heart of the pale blueness of the sky.

I arrived at the last step in the stairway without effort; it was as though something were bearing me along, rather was it that I didn't even feel that something was bearing me along, some power that was outside me yet which, at the same time, emanated from within me. The sea was below me, far away, ever so remote, and the waves were clashing together soundlessly, excessively distant, and the foam, tossed about in a zigzag, slightly frothy line, was melting away in a greeny blueness close to the shore.

The final step was wide and unsupported, creating the impression that one could easily slip and fall, yet it held no danger, not the least threat, as if the descent from it to the surface of the sea that sparkled, deep and unfathomable underneath, would be more like a weightless landing without gravity or shock. Its marble was polished and rounded and contained no little pores, which had gradually decreased the further I climbed, until its full bloom was restored to it, new, warm and utterly smooth.

The sensation of the hot marble had an enjoyment about it; it was as though it were responding, merely through this tender heat, to a particular demand in the body clinging to it, transferring its grateful heat and deferring to its silent, feminine gentleness with a discreet and engrossed enjoyment; an enjoyment that ripples and tumesces and takes in the sky, the distant waters of the sea and the great blaze of the sun quietly burning, cleaving to contours that are easy and pliant, then swirling and massing and swelling till it explodes. The burning disc of the sun flies apart into shreds that are immersed in the belly of the blueness in scattered stabbings with extended echoes and melt away. And the light of noon returns sober, white and silent-coloured.

I came to the end of the street and left behind me the last of the huts. I had the sensation that the blood of youth was still flowing in me for a few final years. From behind the church the railway station appeared small and distant and still, as though it were a toy, and on the other side I could see the topmost tips of a narrow grove of date palms spread out in a curving line, drowning and almost submerged between two undulating dunes of white sand, only the tops of the palm leaves, scarcely stirring, showing above them.

I stood in an expanse of sand that appeared to be unclean: piles of heaped-up litter were scattered about at random, having a smell only of a slightly sickly sweetness. I told myself that where we are concerned our garbage easily disintegrates, for what do we throw away as garbage? And yet I saw red Coca-Cola cans that were flaking, newly imported blue cans of Seven-Up, torn nylon bags with faded advertisements for whisky and cigarettes, the spiky tips of splinters of glass projecting from pages of newspapers and an old torn woman's swimsuit and bits of tattered rags.

At the beginning of the empty space overlooking the stretch of desert, behind the railway lines, stood the huge ten-ton lorries, their enormous wheels of thick black rubber so solidly heavy that a part of them had sunk into the hard sand. Their engines were turning over with a rhythmic rumbling sound. The drivers had left them and were gathered in a small circle, with their imported leather jackets and with their scarves round their powerful necks. One of them was wearing a round white skull-cap over his long hair. They were smoking and from their cigarettes there rose up in the stillness of the wintry summer resort a slightly blue, fragrant smoke. They were not talking.

The lorries were weighed down with mixed loads of cement and books and paper and bricks and iron rods piled up with their ends unevenly stacked; they were of differing lengths and the ends of the thin rods protruded, arching upwards and giving warning of how easily they could pierce and rend. Though I was very far away, I turned my head aside as though to avoid them, and came to a stop.

Not far distant I saw a young police sergeant with a thin athletic body, a cap on his shaved head, his revolver in its dark brown holster. He was standing in a bored attitude, his face motionless with suppressed anger, his eyes not looking at anything. Behind him were two plain-clothes men with long overcoats and high regulation boots; they were bare-headed and each one held a thin cane which he struck against the side of his overcoat with regular movements.

Behind me all the huts were locked; along their fronts had been let down coverings of intertwined matting, fixed to the ground by great iron rings, coarse and rusty, while the wintry setting sun cast long shadows on to the deserted sandy pathways.

As I stood there without moving, I looked around me anxiously. There was no longer anyone but myself at the end of this sandy world; anxiously I waited for someone to come, as though to save me from some danger I didn't know of, for someone to appear and to bring with him – merely by making his appearance – companionship, affection and security, for a voice to be raised, for a cry or a scream. And no one comes.

There is nothing there but the murmur of the sea waves, their relentless rhythm ever repeated, so far away.

The workers from Upper Egypt were circling round the lorries in small groups. They were unloading the stacked-up piles of iron bars, and the iron would fall with a muffled thud, immediately scoring long lines on the sandy ground. Sacks of cement, covered on the outside with their own white dust which had erased the writing on them so that all that showed were the faint letters 'Portland' in English, were being lifted by an Upper Egyptian with a powerful back, who had got into the lorry and had placed an old piece of sacking over himself to protect his head and body. He would let the sacks slide down from his braced back to be snatched up by his fellow workers from below, their arms raised, strained, and they would throw them on to the iron, and from underneath them he would gather up motley piles of books and magazines, and pieces of paper of various shapes and sizes, which he would throw to them, and the books would fall from their hands on to the sand, and the covers, their colours faded, would be ripped apart. In amongst them would fly in all directions sheets of paper, new and shiny and old and yellowed, printed and written in strange handwritings, and on typewriters, as if they were governmental communications or love letters or rough notes taken of lectures, and I saw old numbers of the magazines *al-Fukaha, al-Hilal, Kullu Shayy,* and *al-Muqtataf* and *al-Lata'if al-Musawwara,* and *al-Magalla, al-Katib* and *al-Kawakib,* with their differently sized and variously coloured covers and their nostalgic pictures and drawings. The workers were throwing one pile on top of another so that the books and papers were being crumpled. I had the sensation of the red bricks scraping against their rough hands as they quickly transferred them, four at a time, throwing them on to the books and the cement and the sand and the iron so that thin, brittle chips would break off from their symmetrical edges.

They were all silent. The only sound was that of the iron grating against the side of the lorries as it slid down and hit the sand, the rustling of the papers, and the sound of the sacks of cement rasping against the dryness of the bricks. No one was talking.

I said to myself: 'Where is the joyful singing of the Upper Egyptians with echoes of faraway sadness, when they take up and put down the loads of the world?'

I did not hear the sound of what I had said to myself.

With a burning, irrepressible urge I wanted to approach the circle of drivers. I knew with a knowledge of utter despair that they would not see me, and that if I addressed them they would not hear me. And yet I wanted to move towards them, while my bare feet, wet with sea water, shifted around on the sands, digging, with their slowed, heavy turning, a deep, determined hole, and yet they did not move.

The first tongues of fire rose up from amidst the debris. In the pure air there was an acrid, penetrating smell. The flames advanced slowly, with timorous wariness at first, then writhing with greater confidence and all at once plunging down until they disappeared and no trace was to be seen of them amongst the iron and cement, then suddenly bursting forth, as though from deep within my anxious self, from the other side of the piles, above the bricks whose colour I saw was blackening slightly. And I saw the fires take on their full glory, robustly in command, and there was the sound of them babbling with quick, successive crackings and poppings, with the smoke from the paper giving out a smell of burnt lime.

I saw the red-coloured covers of *Hours of Pride*[1] growing white between the flaming tongues, their white pages folding in upon themselves, curling and falling as the fire consumed them. I heard the voices of old friends I hadn't seen for a long time; among them were some who were now living in London, in Paris and Harvard, and among them was a friend I had loved dearly who had died a short while ago of cancer of the brain, also a friend who had drowned twenty years ago in Agami, and Victoria was running with them in the faded blue fluffy bathrobe. There were many of them and they were running after things that are not easily attained. They were running towards me, towards the fire, and calling out for help, to telephone the fire brigade, and for buckets of sea water, while other voices were saying there was nothing to be done about it.

Then the fires exploded into a roar of radiant light.

Note
1. One of the author's volumes of short stories.

MOHAMMED BARRADA

Life by Instalments

We woke late, yawning as we lay on the bed, our bones feeling as though they'd fall apart. It seemed to us that this day would proceed on its way like its predecessors. We leaned our head against the wooden headboard. Our sight was bleared and no doubt a dark yellowness overspread our face. Having previously visited the doctor, we had submitted our state of health to him and he had shaken his head knowingly:

'You're not alone – all those who think and dream and aren't content with reality are afflicted with your condition.'

We remembered the same answer having been given by a doctor – perhaps by our own doctor himself – to a friend when he complained of indigestion and heartburn.

'Is there a cure, doctor?'

'I shall give you some pills that will do you good, but I don't advise you to be too optimistic. Every morning, on opening your eyes, search around in your mind for some amusing story or event, grin from ear to ear, then leap out of bed and lift up your voice in song – in these circumstances an unpleasant voice is acceptable.'

We wanted to try out the doctor's advice so we searched round in the crevices of our memory for some story that would set us off laughing first thing. Ah yes, we had found it: the story of the foreign neighbour who from time to time amused herself by taking a taxi, despite the fact that she was a car-owner. When the cab arrived at the door of the building she would claim she had forgotten her money at home and that she would go upstairs to bring the man the fare. She would then go up and not return, and the poor man would continue to hoot away and everyone in the building would look down without understanding what he was up to. Of course he wouldn't know the building and would make off in despair, while she would go on laughing her head off inside her room. Ha ha ha! We had our fill of laughing and secretly gave thanks to our clever neighbour, then we jumped out of bed and began a new day in the long holiday.

For a long time we wandered aimlessly round our well-stocked library. We noticed that most of its contents were books we had put off reading and which we had decided to return to when there was sufficient time. Our hand stretched out to a red volume whose author had lived forty years ago in the red city of Marrakesh. It was Mehammed ibn Mohammed ibn Abdullah al-Mu'aqqat's *The Marrakesh Journey or the Temporal Mirror of Vile Deeds,* also called *The Sword Unsheathed against Him Who Renounces the Prophet's Sunna.* [1]

'. . . then after that Sheikh Abdul Hadi said: "And this person asking and the person asked were from among the people of the tenth century, so how much more so in this time of ours which has become like the unbelieving night? As for its leaders, they have brought tyranny to their subjects. They have eaten flesh and drunk blood; they have sucked the marrow from the bone and have swallowed up the brains, leaving people neither the world nor yet religion. As for the things of the world, they have made away with them; and as for religion, they have enticed them from it. This is something we have witnessed, not something we have thought up . . ." '

Abu Zeid asked: 'May Allah give you strength, is it permissible for one to remain in such a place when one is incapable of changing that which is objectionable?'

The mind finds no relaxation in reading: the old appears new, the new old, and the brain shrieks out at the impossibility of this being so, does not accept that 'the sun is blind'. We have told ourselves that the source of all that was perhaps boredom, the length of the association, the unearthing of hidden depths, the exposing of illusions, the scattering of one's dreams, clinging to what is to come and being oblivious of that which exists. Let us then train the soul to patience and let us live the detailed and elaborate present, the daily routine that is repeated.

Our guest at lunch was a relative who was getting on for sixty. He had learnt the Qur'an by heart when young, knowing its every letter, and had eventually become a *muezzin*. When his wife had died a year ago he had chosen a relative of his to get married to, it not being permissible for a *muezzin* to remain unmarried, but he had preferred that the marriage should take place after his return from the Pilgrimage. During his absence busybodies had intervened and the woman had got married to someone else, leaving him with nobody. He is nevertheless still searching for a wife.

'Please Allah, you are well. In all circumstances we give thanks to Him. And how's the health and the work? Fine. May we always be in your prayers. And how is this young lad getting on: Is he making a bit of an effort? Ask him and he'll answer you. For myself I see him as a slacker. Shame on you, my boy. If only you'd model yourself on your uncle Abdurrahman.'

As though his words had awakened some clouded-over memory, we said:

'The one who died of drowning?'

'Yes – and as a martyr too. The Prophetic Tradition singles out three categories of people to be considered martyrs: those who die by fire, those who die by drowning, and those who die by having a wall collapse on top of them.'

He now directed his conversation at the young lad, who showed no annoyance, so used was he to listening to advice and instructions in a variety of shapes and forms.

'Your uncle Abdurrahman had a thorough grasp of all the sciences when he was eighteen years old . . .'

Smiling, the boy interrupted him:

'I'm still no more than seventeen.'

We interposed with due pomposity:

'Your head is emptier than the skull of a donkey. You should put to good account what we are saying to you. The future is yours, and you are the loser if you don't follow our advice. Do you think it's easy to make a living? Some wear decorations round their necks, others a headstall.'

The Hajj continued what he had to say:

'Abdurrahman, may Allah continue to bestow His blessings upon him, was proficient in all the sciences. His handwriting was exceedingly beautiful. He was employed at the Finance Department and donned the *kaftan* and turban when he was still young.

130

He was a great swimmer and an accomplished horseman. One day a jurisprudent who came to visit us from Sousse saw him and was taken by his intelligence and knowledge, especially when he found that he had learnt al-Dumyati by heart. Afraid for him from the envious eyes of man and djinn, he wrote him a charm to wear called "the amulet of the sea and the nullification of hindrances", which he ordered him to hang on his *kaftan* so that no harm might come to him.'

In order to exhibit our interest in the subject, be it only outwardly, we said:

'And despite this amulet he was drowned in the sea?'

'Everything is by divine decree. He was returning from Rabat to Salé and crossed the *wadi* of Abu Raqraq in a boat. He then took off his turban, made his ablutions and performed the mid-day prayer. He later left the place and hadn't gone twenty paces when the idea of having a swim came to him. So, going back to the same place, he took off his clothes and went in to have a swim.'

In the same way, with the same smile, the boy interrupted him:

'Used they to swim in the nude in those days?'

Though we found the question a reasonable one, the situation demanded a different reaction. We therefore looked daggers at him, clapped our hands together in a gesture of despair and made every effort not to burst out laughing.

'No, they used to swim in a loincloth. It happened that day that he had left the amulet in his other *kaftan*. His skill in swimming helped him not and the sea has kept him swallowed up until now.'

Thus did Abdurrahman die and, where the sciences of this world and the next are concerned, it is we who were the losers.

The conversation petered out with the lunch not yet over. We looked at the man as he chewed away leisurely. Was there any other subject we could engage him in? We recollected some of the stories and bits of news he had on numerous occasions recounted to us. It would be sufficient for us to make reference to one of them for him to burst forth in a repetition of what we had already heard. We could for example say: 'By Allah, the people of that time used to do it with real feeling when they called out to their king: "Glory and gold be to Moulay Abdul Aziz," ' for him to tell us again of the battles and skirmishes that took place between Sultan Moulay Abdul Aziz and certain tribes, and he would continue on till he arrived at the time of Bu Hmara and the entry of the French. However, finding that this would be tedious, we thought instead to ask him about his private life: What did he do with himself after giving the call to prayers and performing his prayers? The smoking of hashish he had given up after his return from the Holy Places and the new wife hadn't yet put in an appearance, so how did he pass his time? Did he regard himself as being dead? It seemed that his relationship with the world surrounding him was extremely limited. He would pick up various bits of news, corroborate them and conclude his words with: 'Allah gives a choice and He chooses.'

The boy eats greedily; perhaps he's not thinking about any-thing. He is drawn to what is taking place around him, be it only in a mechanical manner. He has discovered the pleasure of smoking, chasing after the neighbours' daughters, also the foot-ball craze. After some thought he announces his desire to travel to Europe during the summer vacation, even if he has to walk (which would multiply the cost of his pilgrimage).

And we? We think about the old man and the boy, and we make guesses about what may perhaps be filling their minds and about their relationships with what is around them. And after that? The siesta. And then? Wandering around and getting a breath of fresh air. And then? We'll telephone our girlfriend. We'll meet up, we'll chatter away, our temperature will rise, our instincts burst forth. Boredom will take over again. We'll part. We'll meet up with some friends. We'll talk about everything. We'll criticize. We'll commend. We'll show displeasure. Enthusiasm will vanish when we see the extent of our impotence. We'll set off anew into the street. We'll feel lust renewing itself through the vibrations of the rounded and curved portions of women's bodies. Always we used to ask our married friends: 'Does it mean that your wife acts as a representative for her sex?' We get the answer: 'Not at all, there is no one who desires other women more than married men, even though we love our wives.' We try to comprehend the question, to rationalize it. No doubt it's due to the mixing of the sexes, to provocative advertising, to make-up, to high heels and . . . and what else?

We told him that and he interrupted us sharply:

'That's rubbish. With love we can overcome the infatuation of sex.'

'And where is love?'

'Ah, you're one of those pessimistic types. I'll tell you my story.' Of course his story is run-of-the-mill: they wanted to marry her off to an old man, so she threatened to commit suicide and the two of them pledged themselves to love each other until death etc.

He won't understand us then – no point in repeating to him what Freud said: 'I am accustoming myself to the idea of regarding every sexual act as a process in which four persons are involved.'

We exaggerate and the moment grips and imprisons us. It is not the infatuation of sex alone that threatens or tempts us. There is the infatuation of crime, of suicide, of drink, of revolt. The other categories do not greatly tempt us because they do not destroy the familiar. And writing?

'And I was silent and no answer was seen from him and he started to tell his beads. Abdul Basit said to him: "Master, I have always known about you that you possess a tongue that renders the most eloquent speechless and dazzles their minds . . . You embolden us morning and eve with those treatises that captivate the heart, leaving in our souls its delectable mark. It is thus that I used to know you, so how about you now?" '

In the evening we were conscious of the same feeling of disintegration in our bones, also an even gloomier melancholy. We thought of ridding ourselves of it through the same famous medical prescription, but we hesitated because the doctor was precise about determining the time it should be taken: in the morning, not the evening. We shall wander round the streets, we shall scrutinize people's facial expressions that perchance we may hit upon the remedy. We walked for a long time: the cafés are full, the bottles of beer are emptied in a flash, laughter rings out, the never-slackening rattle of fruit machines. Even so our melancholy persists, will not let up. The cars fly past, the buses are slow, jam-packed, the cinemas advertise their heroes. It appeared to us that everyone around us was running away, and it occurred to us to stop them, to shout at them: 'You're running away.' But the idea seemed fatuous, unsupported by any basis.

133

We asked ourselves: Is there anything that endures? Then we returned home to write the story of this life we live by instalments.

Note
1. *The Sayings of the Prophet Mohammed.*

YUSUF ABU RAYYA

Dreams Seen by a Blind Boy

It's a Friday and the blind boy is in the company of his mother on the road to the graveyards. In the graveyards are mourning women with grandfathers and fathers and mothers and husbands and sons in the earth.

In the Qur'an, which the blind boy has learnt by heart, there is compassion for all.

His mother sits him down where the women want and he recites: 'Say: He, Allah is One, Allah the Everlasting Refuge . . .' Then he recites: 'Say: I take refuge with the Lord of mankind, the King of mankind . . .'

He receives bread, leavened and unleavened, and his mother doesn't take him back to the house until her baskets are filled. On other days his mother would take him in the mornings to the Sheikh where he would recite, with the rest of the boys, verses from the Qur'an; he would hear too about the life of the Prophet and would learn that the Prophet was born a child like every other child and that he was poor and an orphan. When, though, he became a man he had said to his people: 'Your gods are of stone, but Allah is the Light of the heavens and the earth,' and he said to the slaves: 'Men are equal like the teeth of a comb.' He rode a strong horse, in his hand a sword of fire, and he led them to where he killed ignorance and built for people a shining city.

The Sheikh, though, would strike him with the wide piece of wood when he made a mistake in repeating things about the Prophet's life. They were not in his mind as the Sheikh would have liked but were down in the depths of his heart, aglow with soft and joyous light. They would glow too during his night of dreams when he would see the Prophet in his white robe riding on his white horse, in his hand the green standard and the gleaming sword. And he, the young blind child, would see, between the horse's legs, the light and the horse's shadow on the yellow sand, and he would stretch out his little hand wanting to grasp the standard with the three stars, or the sword that sparkled in the sunlight.

At other times he would see himself wearing a flowing robe, on his head a red tarboosh with a black tassel, standing on the high pulpit, the people wide-eyed in front of him, saying things to them that illuminated their hearts, that shed green light for them on their paths.

Then he is standing in the prayer niche, decorated with designs and Qur'anic verses, with the people behind him, rising to their feet as he rises, bowing in prayer as he bows. He says: 'Not of those You are angry against, nor of those that are astray,' and with the voice of a single strong man they reply: 'Amen.'

At last he awakes, opens his eyes and finds that they are still looking at everlasting darkness.

Benumbed by the night's dream, he gets up and performs his ablutions. Feeling with his stick along the ground, he makes his way to the nearby mosque where he stands behind the Imam and intones with the people: 'Amen.' When the sun shines and the people are moving about in the streets, his mother takes him to the Sheikh where he slips in between the other boys, recites verses from the Qur'an and listens to the life of the Prophet. On Fridays he recites to the dead so that the baskets may be filled with leavened and unleavened bread.

ABDEL-HAKIM KASSEM

The Trial of the Small Black Woman

The Case

He gave a troubled sigh.

'I didn't kill her!'

He slightly loosened the woollen muffler round his neck to ease his breathing. People said about this muffler that it was eating into his neck, which day by day was getting more emaciated. They were all going to the ceremony held after her funeral. He was conscious of their jostling footsteps, their breathing and the rustling of their *galabias* around him. Returning from the evening prayer, cold and fear stung him and he clung to the muffler enveloping his neck like a hangman's noose. He was assailed by a fit of coughing that almost brought his eyes out of their sockets.

'I didn't kill her!'

The coughing all but thrust his soul out from his chest. He leaned against a wall for a while to regain his breath. His tear-filled eyes weren't seeing what was around him, yet he proceeded slowly to the ceremony.

From underneath his eyebrows he let his eyes roam over the silent, bowed heads. He squinted warily in the direction of the Qur'an reciter. His eye-sockets were deep, obliterated by the shadows. The blind face filled him with fear. He brought his head down between his shoulders. Her face too was frightening. Her legs were thin, like two pieces of iron. She would hobble when she walked. He shivered as though hearing her halting footsteps pursuing him in the darkness of the lane the night his money was stolen.

That night, feeling the pocket of his *galabia,* he had not found the money tied up in the handkerchief. He had turned round in terror, screaming: 'Woman, you've stolen my money!'

Her eyes had gleamed in the darkness like two knives and he shrank before her anger. She had screamed at him: 'Get away from me, cursed be your father, with your filthy money!'

He was choking. He held his breath. His gaze became fixed on the Qur'an reciter with the frightening appearance. More coughing assailed him, tearing at his chest. The faces of those attending the ceremony turned in his direction and the reciter fell silent as he took his cough outside in his search for fresh air. Leaning against a wall, he went on coughing till his body grew cold, the tips icy, and he felt his head clearing. He collapsed to a sitting position beside the wall.

The night he had lost his money he had gone to the Imam of the mosque and had wept before him:

'She was walking in the lane at my heels. The bundle of money fell from me. For certain she picked it up. She's the guilty one, not a doubt of it.'

The Imam of the mosque had lowered his head for a while, then said:

'Let the Sheikh of the *mandal*[1] with his God-inspired knowledge decide about the matter.'

The Judgment

The Imam of the mosque was tortured with pain before being able to get up from his sitting position on the bench. Tall and lean, he was like a stick of sugar cane. He opened wide his legs: the thing hanging down between his thighs impeded him painfully. His face was as yellow as that of a dead man, his eyes swollen. As he left the ceremony he proceeded with short, unsteady steps like a child learning to walk.

He sensed the mourners' eyes at his back and the droning of the blind Qur'an reciter's voice. Frightened. He wasn't yet used to the darkness of the street, the corners alive with weird mysteries. He shrank into himself as he took stumbling steps. Bold glimmerings of light rose amidst the darkness. Fear ran through his limbs as he imagined eyes gleaming with pronouncements of guilt. He almost died of fright. He made an effort to stir the lifelessness of his lips. The words issued tremblingly from his mouth. 'The Verse of the Chair'[2] brought peace to his heart and he went on reciting it, holding fast to the words.

Oh, the mystery of words! His whispered reciting grew louder, the shakings of his head more pronounced. A feeling of sadness flooded his soul and his tears, copious and abject, flowed down. How often had he stayed up alone at night! How often had the mystery of words kept him awake! Yet they understood not, these peasants, these cattle with hearts that were blind.

His eyes got used to the darkness and he was able to see. He stood leaning on his stick, gaunt, his legs apart, looking ahead of him with diseased eyes, while around him stood the mud huts, brown and silent, the sticks of firewood with the fringes heavy with dew, hanging down. He whispered, addressing the mud huts as though seeing them seated on the mats of the mosque:

'She had the eyes of an insolent devil. She would hop along like a monkey. Never was she a godly woman – firewood for Hellfire. Allah pronounced His word against her because she had stolen.'

The Implementation

All the people came. There was a great noise. The Imam of the mosque stood there, gaunt, legs apart, leaning on his stick amidst the circle of people with alongside him the Sheikh of the *mandal*. The latter raised his arms aloft and the people fell completely silent. Stretching out his hand, he seized a young boy by the wrist. The boy almost died of fright. The owner of the *mandal* placed on the small outstretched palm a brand new pitcher that had never been moistened by water. Leaving the pitcher on the boy's quivering, outstretched hand, he raised his arms, his face skywards, and began reciting strange words that were intelligible to no one. His face was frighteningly emaciated. He screamed at those present:

'Let the thief confess his crime before he is exposed. If not the pitcher will recognize him through the mystery of words, through the mystery of the *mandal*.'

Silence hung like a dome raised above the mud headstones of graves.

The pitcher began to shake, to dance, to sway, with the boy being guided by it through his thin arm. It took him into the alleyway, the people behind it, a silent, gaping throng, right up to the house of the small black woman, a house like an animal's burrow, without livestock or children.

No sooner had the pitcher come to rest at the house than the people gave a shout: the single shout of a beast ravenous for its prey. The woman clung to the wall, screaming in terror. The Imam of the mosque went up to her:

'Return the money to its owner, thief!' and the shouting of the gathering of people was behind him: 'Thief! Thief!'

The small black woman went on with her terrified, anguished wailing.

The people went back to the open space at the top of the alleyway. They all stood in a circle round the Imam of the mosque and the Sheikh of the *mandal*. The latter produced a waterskin which, slowly, unhurriedly, he went on blowing up; very gradually it became inflated, assuming the form of some bloated dead animal.

'Hang up this waterskin,' the Sheikh of the *mandal* addressed the people, 'in the house of godly folk and its curse will fall upon the thief. It will swell and she will suffer torment until death.'

And so it was. In this form, in the form of a bloated dead animal, the small black woman was found dead in her house after not being seen for several days, during which time she had kept wholly to her house.

Thus did she die, and here are the men at her funeral, with bowed heads listening to the Qur'an being recited by the blind youth with hollows for eyes.

The Truth of the Matter

The woman was good: black, small and good. No one had known whose daughter she was, nor to whom she was related. She just was: a solitary cactus that no one knew who had planted. Yet she was good, laughing and crying as children do and, like a cat, scratching anyone who harmed her. She would spend all day long wandering through the lanes collecting up corn cobs that had fallen from the camels carrying them and gathering up dung and firewood as fuel for her stove.

And he? There is no power or strength except through God. What was it possible for him to do? The money had been in his pocket all the time. The stolen money was wrapped round in the handkerchief and was tied with two knots. But, O Protector, what was it possible for him to do?

His eyes were closed, his head bowed, and the voice of the Qur'an reciter came to him from far off. It was as though God were censuring him, as though the unlawful bundle of money in his pocket were pulling at him, dragging him down to Hell's punishment. The people were greatly perturbed by the affair, while he sat rigid and paralysed. From the moment he had picked up the bundle of money from the ground in the darkness of the alley, he had been rigid and paralysed, unable to find the courage to do anything.

He looked towards the man who was coughing so hard. He wished with all his heart that his soul might depart from him with one of those coughs of his, that devil of a money-lender. What loss was it to him if the money in the handkerchief were lost to him when he had, in the aperture in his wall, a whole jugful of pound notes? How delighted he'd been when he'd picked the knotted handkerchief off the ground by the foot of that dog of a man. He now grasped the bundle of money so tightly it hurt; the palm of his hand was wet with sweat.

On the day of the *mandal* he had gone with the people to witness it. The knotted handkerchief had been in his pocket, his hand gripping it. The pitcher had passed by him. It was as though he had died a thousand deaths by a blunt axe. But the pitcher had passed by him and had made its way towards her house. O Protector! How unfortunate are the weak, the unsupported, the resourceless!

What could he do? The waterskin had been hung up in the middle of the house of a godly man and the people were not sleeping for terror, while he had sat in his hallway with open mouth and open eyes, motionless and unblinking, until the shrieking of the women had announced her death and the village had given a sigh of relief. Now here he was at her funeral with the voice of the Qur'an reciter coming to him like a lamentation for the dead.

Lamentation swept through him. Terror crushed him. His flesh oozed sweat as though he were ill with a thousand ailments that were alien to physicians. He jumped to his feet and set off, heedless of everything, to the money-lender's house. He was squatting in the middle of the floor coughing, distracted from everything around him by his coughing. Throwing the knotted handkerchief of money into his lap, he fled. No one had recognized him.

People Forget

The scorchingly hot days of summer have soft late afternoons. At the time of the afternoon prayer the open space at the top of the lane was a playground for fresh breezes. The seller of cloth comes and undoes his bundle, revealing dresses of brilliant colours. The women are all round him, letting out gurgling ripples of laughter.

At the time of the afternoon prayer there comes the seller of water jugs, that forward fellow, black of arm and thigh, with a great head to him and a great sex. He sets the jugs up around him as though they are silent black children. That forward fellow flirts with the women as, in fits of laughter, they surround him.

And in the depths of the houses they strip naked. The warm water flows from the jugs, daringly stinging bare bodies. Under the effect of the water on their bodies, shudderings and moanings break forth. Then the groups of women make off to where the zar[3] ritual is being held, where they dance to the savage rhythm of the drums in their coloured *galabias* until they enter a state of trance. They had escorted her bier up to the end of the lane and had shrieked behind it until they had no breath left.

Notes
1. The practice of magic through the contemplation of a mirror-like surface generally performed through a boy acting as a medium.
2. One of the verses of the Qur'an most often recited.
3. A ritual dance, accompanied by drumming, performed by women for exorcizing a devil.

142

MOHAMMED CHUKRI

Flower Crazy

Outside in the lane the children are yelling.

She wakes and sits up. With legs dangling over the side of the bed, she bends her head forward. The two of them are eating bread dipped in oil and drinking cold green tea left by their mother in the pot. They look at her as they chew. Lost in thought, dizzy, she takes her head in her hands and presses down on it. Rising unsteadily, a hand over her mouth, she goes to the lavatory. Its loathsome smell helps her to be violently sick: viscid, yellow vomit. The sound of her vomiting is choked like that of an animal being slaughtered. Her elder brother brings her a plastic bucket containing some water. She drops back exhausted on the bed. She is sobbing. The younger brother goes out, the other is sitting silently in front of her. She sits up and they exchange glances sadly. Her lustreless eyes water with tears. She smiles. They both smile. With a movement of head and hands she invites him over, seats him alongside her, hugs him to her breast, smiling; smiling, she takes his small face in her hand; smiling, she wipes away the trickle of his tears.

The children outside are playing ball and yelling. She gives him a coin. He smiles. He kisses her cheek and goes out.

Outside in the lane misery is more friendly to young and old. There beauty looks out curiously from small, gloomy doorways. It is the same beauty as is sold on the streets of the new city.

The crippled poet of the quarter is a witness to what has happened ever since all the people of this lane were living in shacks. He teaches the young and the old, for a fee or for thanks; he reads and writes lovers' letters; he gives support to the ailing by reciting the Qur'an, to love through poetry; he plays with the children and sits of an evening with the old men.

A child eats bread and chocolate. She is sitting on the doorstep of her house looking out at the goings-on of the lane. She savours what she is eating. A little boy in front of her has a red flower in his hand. Its stalk dances between his thin, dirty fingers. The hunger in his eyes woos the bread. She stops eating, the chunk of bread close to her mouth. He is looking at the flower, smelling it, while he smiles at her enticingly. The dance of hunger lies in his eyes, his legs, his hands, his whole body. Her dreamy eyes ask for his dancing flower. His hand is stretched towards his mouth, hers towards her nose.

She gets up and drains the pot into one of the two greasy glasses and sips at the dregs. She rubs her eyes and takes from her handbag a packet of Virginian cigarettes. Sitting on the bed, she lights one. She looks at the picture of her father in a small dilapidated frame on the oozing wall. She smokes, looking at the picture of her father. She coughs violently. She remembers her father's cough and the threads of blood he would spit out. Again she feels dizzy and gets up, coughing and throwing away half of her cigarette, to go to the lavatory. Straining, she vomits a thin thread of spittle. She is reminded of the spittle of drunks, their senseless chatter and their violence amidst the clamour of the singing and fog of smoke. She looks into a small mirror hanging near her head. Her night face has the colour of oil; it is puffy, the eyes bleary. She clasps her hands in front of her, then presses down on her shoulder muscles with repeated movements, her chest shaking and thrust forward. She feels her breasts and finds them firm. Sighing, seated on the bed, she opens her legs, then scratches at the bush of hair that she has not shaved for a long time. She loves to see her nakedness through her own eyes, much more than through the eyes of men.

Flower Crazy. This is how the people of the quarter have called him. The crippled poet is a witness. Flower Crazy lives with his mother in a hut. Every morning they go together to the city, only returning at evening. She begs and he distributes his flowers amongst the beautiful women and girls. He asks nothing of them. He buys his flowers with his mother's money or he steals them. He has been arrested and sent to court many times but, through pity for his madness for flowers, he is let off. His last flower he always throws to the woman living on the ground floor.

Once, out of sympathy for his madness for flowers, she threw him her handkerchief. That night he dreamed of gardens of flowers that he would pick with mad joy and of handkerchiefs that fell upon him from the window of the handkerchief woman. The day of the handkerchief is better than a thousand days. Peace she is, the woman, after the day of the handkerchief. So did he start talking to those he knew. He began to date his life as from the day of the handkerchief: this happened before the day of the handkerchief, this after the day of the handkerchief. Even women before the handkerchief were not the same as after the handkerchief. No longer did he give his flowers to all women. The bunch that had been bought or stolen was for the woman of the handkerchief. His coming with the flowers and her presence at the window was the promise of a rendezvous between them. When the husband was cured of his cold, he smelt Flower Crazy's smell on his wife's body. When the husband was cured of his eye ailment, he saw Flower Crazy leaping from the window and his wife nimbly going out of the door and running after Flower Crazy. He was too fat to run after them.

She made up her night face, putting blue drops into her eyes; she exuded an aroma of costly perfume. From her small ward-robe she took out an expensive dress, more diaphanous, sleek and clinging than all her other dresses, and a pair of beautiful, silver-coloured shoes with high heels which she wrapped up in the pages of a foreign magazine she had bought both for her new and her old shoes. She put on an old pair of shoes and carried the new under her arm. Before going out she cast a glance at her large, beautifully dressed doll she had bought with her own money when she had grown up and begun to earn.

Her younger brother is sitting by the doorstep playing with a kitten and a paper ball tied to a string, while in front of him is an emaciated dog lying in the shade overcome by sleep and fatigue. Leaving the kitten, he comes to say goodbye to her. She gives him a small coin and kisses him. He asks her to come back early in the evening, before he goes to sleep. Her other brother is far away, playing football with the team of youngsters from the lane. Women and children are drawing water amidst curses and clamour at the hydrant for the lane. A child excretes near the hedge, then scratches at the excrement with a small stick and smells it. A lank dog hovers around; its eyes widen, its tail wags. Two young girls insult one another where their buckets lie in a row. One of them has lifted her dress, exposing her naked bottom, and says to her rival in the queue around the hydrant:

'You're no more than that to me.'

The other exposes her front to her, then they both start slapping each other, pulling at each other, shouting insults. Some young men seated on the ground, leaning against the wall, and listlessly smoking, look on derisively at what is happening. One of the young men whistles at her in mock flirtation and two children beg money from her. She gives them two coins and goes on her way through the mud, distressed and miserable. Some of the looks she gets are of admiration, some of hate and envy.

Near the entrance to the muddy lane she hides the worn-out shoes and puts on the new ones, then walks along the asphalt road to the new town.

The crippled poet of the lane writes about these things that go on in the lane, also about things in the town, things he hasn't lived through or seen but has heard of from those who have seen them or related them. These are some of his memoirs:

Yesterday I thought anew about my life through zeros. From the right to the left I thought of the value of zeros. I thought of everything through nothing. 'He will not be questioned about what He does but they will be questioned.' What befalls you from the right is from Allah and what befalls you from the left is from yourself. Allah divides and you multiply but you do not act equitably and Allah is best at acting equitably in computation. To destroy all idols – that is what you know. But Allah does not plot against you if you should do away with what you built for yourselves.

Sex! Sex! Sex! This is your misfortune, so seek the happiness of the Promise if you are steadfast believers. I am angry at this human hunger that does not cease till death. I no longer remember my pride which used to prevent me from loving. Sweet distance was my sole solace. The debauchery that is stronger within me than the chastity always gets the better of me. Never did she who at the time I desired come to me. That one you grieve at parting from and are wearied by her staying on. Beauty! Oh for the beauty that tears at me and is possessed by someone else, someone who mocks me. I have not understood a single woman other than in spurts of imagination: in sips, not at one gulp. Maybe I have thought about them all. My desires were divided amongst them. The life I thought about I haven't lived. Ask that one who has lived it, not thought about it.

It is the confession of the final glass, the final friend to leave me. Ask that one who is separated from his homeland. I have a friend who, like me, is overwhelmed by beauty; he hates me in the eyes of his wife and loves me in the eyes of those women who pass through my life. Ask that one who has wearied of the familiar face. Under compulsion I circumambulated the Kaaba, trailing a woman for three whole days, and after her I no longer circumambulated for more than a day of its sun or its moon. The contract of consummation is the whole token of esteem of that friend, while for me it was a subject of talk at the end of the night, the final glass, the final insolvency. Ever averse to performing the obligatory prayers, who can blame me or judge me about the additional ones? We are brothers in the exercise of the power of choice, enemies in compulsion.

Like me the bachelors of this town have become addicted to the night and to the glass of wine, or to merit in the Hereafter or to emigrating before reaching thirty, fleeing from madness, ignorance and death. Today I am alone with my glass, like those who escape to the bars or the brothels in the hope of retrieving some of their bachelorhood. They glorify drink in the evening, curse it in the morning. Every soul will taste of its sweetness and splendour and of its curse. But in all the brothels I have found my sisters and my friends' sisters. I have seen the delirium of night melting away their make-up and ripping off their masks, while, in the prime of youth, their teeth are being eaten away with decay. I have heard them recalling the purity of their childhood in school songs that have been truncated in their recollection, have been re-enacted in romantic novels, films of love, and old and recent memories.

In the main street she enters the bank. She takes out a cheque from her beautiful and expensive leather bag and with difficulty, her hand trembling, signs her name. The cashier looks with curiosity at the cheque and at her. She draws out two hundred dirhams and leaves in confusion. At a shop she buys an illus-

147

trated women's magazine and a packet of gold-tipped cigarettes.

In the tea salon of Madame Porte the beautiful waitress comes to her and stands waiting politely. She knows how generous she is with her. In a voice flawed by the hoarseness of the night's fatigue, she says:

'Bring me an orange juice, cold milk, and toast with butter and jam.'

In the Grand Socco her mother calls out, her eyes on the security guard who chases away women peddlers like herself:

'Onions! Radishes! Oranges!'

In the lane her footballer brother shouts:

'Goal!'

The younger brother is playing with the kitten near the crippled poet of the lane, and the emaciated dog slumbers in front of them, while a child with a dying sparrow in his hand deliberately pees on the shoes she has left in the hedge.

GAMIL ATIA IBRAHIM

The Old Man

The old man is in the corner of the room. His period of service in the government has come to an end and the procedures and papers for retirement are being completed. While in the service and at an age of over fifty he had graduated in law, but in terms of promotion he had not benefited greatly from the qualification. Without uttering a word, the man runs his eyes over the men and women working there.

When he had entered the faculty of law he had been pre-occupied by the question of justice. Why should his wife have died when she was still young? Why had she not given him any children? Was he entitled to have divorced her? Why did she die during the air-raids on Cairo in 1956?

The doctor had told him that the war had frightened her and had affected her weak heart. He was, however, not entirely sure about that because in the last two weeks her state of health had been extremely bad.

The burial grounds of the Imam Shafie in Cairo are full of the living who have taken up residence in the rooms specially built for those visiting the dead. At the time he told himself that directly the war ended he would move her body to the burial grounds of Port Said, but till now he had not carried out his promise.

He had learnt during his long life in government service that nothing was so harmful to an employee as becoming attached to a young girl at work.

He speaks to himself, addressing the depths of his soul, and sees himself standing on a high rock in a wasteland and talking to a group of people, declaiming at them and shouting for justice. He would have liked to have donned a judge's robes and have dispensed justice amongst people. He keeps control of himself, paying particular attention to his hands lest he wave them about in the air as he shouts silently and draws to himself the gaze of those sitting in the room. One hand he puts in a pocket and the other under his chin as he sits relaxed, gazing ahead of him and leaning back against the chair.

He too had been a young man. His wife had been in her prime when he had married her. Later on everyone would say: An old man whose wife had died and who remained a widower the rest of his life, then he went mad during the few hours before he was to go on pension. Let him go off to the lavatory and talk to himself there to his heart's content.

The woman who was deputy head of the department suddenly said to him in a voice that betrayed a dislike of him:

'Mr Abdul Azeem, you can leave. You are now on pension.'

The man realized what was going on in her mind. He decided to ignore her invitation to go, to be driven away from the office. He took refuge in silence and, as usual, did not turn his face to her. Everyone was sitting and looking at him. They all knew that today he would be going back home and would not again put in an appearance. He had retired on pension – and Leila too knew that.

The man began asking himself why he hadn't yet moved his wife's body to the burial grounds in Port Said. Leila wished him good health and a long and happy life, and he said to her, 'That's life.' He wasn't, though, altogether sure that he had said anything to her or whether he hadn't contented himself with looking at her, with staring into her ever-radiant face.

Before leaving the room and saying goodbye to the others he told himself that he hadn't failed his wife, for after the 1956 war there'd been the 1967 war in which both the dwellings of Port Said and its burial grounds had been laid waste, then had come the war of 1973 which had ended with the liberation of part of Sinai, and it hadn't been possible for him throughout these wars to move the body. He also told himself that it was just as well for there were still many wars to come.

HABIB SELMI

Distant Seas

Because we dreamed of distant seas, there were the three of us, Majid, Yassin and I.

We would go down the sandy track when the glare of the sun rose in the vast expanse, and there would come to us the smell of rank water as we approached the well.

We would hear weak and faint the lowing of the calves that had lost their way in the river beds.

Climbing the large olive trees, we would be able to see the river as it dipped down to the south. Always we would stop to view the smoke ascending from the piles of straw that had been collected into large stacks, and we would see frightening forms in that smoke.

Yassin got to know Maryam and he fell in love with her and she with him. She would waylay him every evening in front of the graveyard to give him some almonds, and Majid and I would be pained and would envy Yassin. We decided to steal the almonds from Maryam's field and we began going there every evening stealthily, but Maryam would always be there guarding the trees and chopping off leaves for the cattle. One day, having dressed up in old black clothing and blackened our faces with charcoal and smeared our hands and feet with mud, we went off to the field. As we reached it we saw Maryam; she was sitting on the ground with an olive twig in her hand. We began making weird noises and Maryam became frightened and ran out of the field, at which we went in and filled our pockets with almonds and oranges. When we came out Yassin blocked our way and discovered our theft. He wanted to catch hold of us but we threw him to the ground and kicked him till he was streaming in blood, then we fled. When we had gone very far away, we decided to hide so that his father wouldn't find us and we went to the ravine near the *wadi* and hid ourselves amongst the boulders.

'We'll sleep over there,' he said to me as we went.

I was afraid he'd despise me or hit me or seize my almonds from me if I were to tell him I was frightened of the darkness, so I agreed. We walked along a path that was full of thorns and rocks. When we reached the ravine, we started to cut grass and to remove the straw that was piled up on the ground. The sun had not yet set; the colour of the clouds had changed and the earth behind us looked red.

When night descended we stretched out on the ground and talked about Maryam and Yassin. A short while passed and then we heard a howling from afar.

In order to put my mind at rest Majid said:

'The wolves don't come here because of the many fishermen.'

For a long time we remained silent. Night filled up the ravine and outside the darkness thickened on the ground. I felt that something was moving alongside me and I drew my legs up to my stomach and made myself smaller. Majid was motionless. I punched him but he didn't move. I imagined that he had been bitten by a snake and had died. I crept out of the ravine and fled.

When we met up again I was afraid. I believed that he would hit me but he didn't do so. He shook me by the hand warmly and gave me some of the almonds he still had in his pocket. After that we talked about Maryam and the ravine in which we had hidden, about the night and darkness and about Yassin, and we decided, after a long discussion, to pay him a visit.

We went to him at noon. His mother met us and made much of us; doubtless she didn't know it was we who had beaten him. She led us to his room and sat us down on beautiful wooden chairs. When he saw us Yassin too was delighted and asked his mother to get us something to drink, then he led us to the garden where he showed us the pigeons, rabbits and chickens.

We reached the sixth form. Yassin, having passed the examination, journeyed to the city and we ceased to have any news of him. Majid became a secretary in a leading trading company, then was promoted and became rich. As for Maryam, she married a large landowner, gave birth to several children, then died. I meanwhile remained close to the land, to the trees and birds, and became a hunter. From the city I bought a gun and cartridges and leather boots to protect me from the thorns and rocks.

I shot a pigeon and I shot a fox and I shot a wolf.

All that has passed away and nothing of it remains but faint pictures that gather in the memory like a strong pulse-beat. This happens when I shoot some large bird or stand in front of an almond tree to gaze at its white flowers.

IBRAHIM ASLAN

The Little Girl in Green

Mohammed Effendi Rasheedi went up on to the roof of the house and looked down at his son's car parked in front of the door and at Umm Husein the grocer who was busy selling bread.

Raising his pate with its scanty hair, Mohammed Effendi saw the roofs of the houses, empty except for the lines of washing hung out, and he told himself that that ass of a woman Umm Husein had blocked the whole street with baskets and that if there was a car wanting to pass through and go to the *souk* she'd have to get up and drag the baskets right along to the shop's doorway. He inclined his head till he was able to see Fadlallah Othman Lane from where it began. When he found it empty, with no car approaching, he felt annoyed. He left where he was and stood in front of the dusty prickly pear in the roof-top corner. He saw that its earth had grown dry and cracked in its round clay jar. He thought of going to the bathroom and filling a large glass from the tap to water it with. He went down the stairs at his own pace, without turning to the open door of his flat. Arriving at the ground floor, he stood before the partly open entrance and stretched out his finger and tapped on the closed glass panel.

'Come in, whoever's knocking.'

Mohammed Effendi put the palm of his hand on the door and gently pushed it, listening to its slow creaking. He remained standing there till his eyes grew accustomed to the darkness and he saw the sofa to the right and the old lady sitting on the edge of it to this side, then he went forward and seated himself on the other sofa. He arranged the folds of his *galabia* in his lap and said: 'Good evening, Mrs Umm Abduh.'

'Greetings, Mr Mohammed. Welcome.' She looked with her tiny eyes at the chain of the metal watch fixed to the buttonhole and hanging on to his chest and said that none of the children was there. 'Otherwise they'd have made you a glass of tea.'

'It's not necessary. Just a couple of words and the reply to go with them.'

'All's well, I hope.'

Mohammed Effendi raised his face to the picture of the late Mohammed Effendi Othman hanging on the old wall, then he looked at his feet and asked her if she knew that they had bought a 128 car, to which Mrs Umm Abduh said: 'Why, of course,' and she informed him that she had met Umm Islah[1] in the skylight area when she was giving water to the chickens and she'd congratulated her, 'the very next day'.

Mohammed Effendi said he'd heard of that: 'But I was very annoyed when I found that your son was letting out the air from the tyre.'

'My son?'

'Every blessed day.'

'I wonder which one of them it could be: Abdul Raheem, Husein or Muhsin?'

'Whichever one of them.'

However Mrs Umm Abduh said: 'How can that be seeing that each one of them lives in his own house with his wife and children?'

'But they visit you.'

'Even so, Abu Islah,[2] they're grown-up men.'

Mohammed Effendi said: 'Abdul Raheem, Husein and Muhsin are like our own children and if it was a question of a day or two, I'd say, "So what? – let them play as they like." ' Then he added: 'It's been going on too long, because it's a 128 car and its motor is set crossways. It's actually a private car and anyone seeing it in front of the door would say it was a private car, but we're intending to turn it into a taxi and get it done up, and that's something that'll need a lot of money. It might take a month or a year, or God knows how long. And naturally it's quite disgraceful of them to go on all this time letting the air out of the tyre and our pumping it up, and they letting it out and our pumping it up.'

Mrs Umm Abduh got up from the sofa saying that such talk was quite wrong and that he'd gone too far, and she hurried out of the living-room. Standing in the skylight area, she raised her head and kept calling: 'Umm Islah. Hey, Umm Islah.'

Mohammed Effendi left her still calling and went out of the flat. He descended the few steps and stood in the doorway by the back of the parked car and saw the young girl in her green silk *galabia* sitting alongside the front wheel. She had in her hand a wooden matchstick which she was pressing into the inside of the valve. The compressed air was gushing out and causing her to close her eyes and making her soft hair blow out. He set about crossing the street slowly. He stood in front of Umm Husein the grocer who was putting some money down the front of her dress.

'Good morning, Mrs Umm Husein.'

Umm Husein took hold of the nearest loaf and threw it to the other side of the basket: 'Welcome.'

'The girl is your son Husein's daughter – every blessed day she lets the air out of the tyre.'

Umm Husein looked in the direction of the girl and said: 'Hit her.'

'No, Mrs Umm Husein, before doing any such thing there are grown-up people one should refer to, and you're now the main person in charge of the shop.'

'And if I'm the main person in charge of the shop, should I leave the buying and selling and go running off after a little girl?'

'That's all very well, Mrs Umm Husein, but what's to be done?'

'I'm telling you but you don't want to know: when you find her at it, get hold of her and wring her neck.' Then she called out: 'Get out from where you are, girl – I really don't know what you find so fascinating about that old wreck.'

The little girl got to her feet and ran off laughing. Mohammed Effendi said that if it were a question of a day or two he'd let her play around as much as she liked but that it had been going on for a long time: 'Mrs Umm Abduh is completely in the picture.' He turned towards the other direction of Fadlallah Othman Lane and said: 'Has there been the call to noon prayers yet?'

Umm Husein said she hadn't heard it: 'It's enough to turn your brain inside out.'

Mohammed Effendi turned round and entered the house. Gently he stretched out his hand and pushed the wooden door that was still slightly open, listening to its slow creaking. He saw

Mrs Umm Abduh sitting on the edge of this side of the sofa and the border of the frame of the picture of the late Mohammed Effendi Othman; then, raising his *galabia,* he made his way up the stairs till he reached the roof. The son of his daughter Islah had raised his *galabia* above his small, extended stomach and was standing peeing on the prickly pear. 'Ah, you little wretch!' The boy ran off laughing, without lowering the *galabia* or ceasing to pee. Mohammed Effendi continued to watch him in silence, then once again moved towards the roof wall. He looked down at Fadlallah Othman Lane and saw the car parked in front of the door and Umm Husein the grocer, and he spotted the young girl coming over there. He immediately drew back and hid himself out of sight. He thought he'd let her be until she felt secure and started playing about with the tyre, then he'd go to the bathroom and fill the large glass from the tap and pour it down on top of her. He gazed at the dusty prickly pear and saw the marks of urine spattered on the plump leaves so that their colour showed up. He told himself that she was now sitting on the ground in her green silk *galabia* holding a matchstick and the compressed air would be gushing out and making her soft hair blow out. He nodded his head in confirmation and approached on tiptoe until he was against the roof wall. Mohammed Effendi Rasheedi leaned over all of a sudden, but he was quite unable to see her.

Notes
1. Mohammed Effendi Rasheedi's wife. Literally 'the mother of Islah'.
2. 'Father of Islah', i.e. Mohammed Effendi Rasheedi.

ZAKARIA TAMER

Small Sun

Abu Fahd was returning home. He walked with slow steps, swaying slightly, through the narrow winding alleys that were lit by widely scattered lamps giving out a yellow light.

The silence that reigned all round him oppressed Abu Fahd, so he began to sing in a soft lilting voice:

'Poor me, what a state I'm in!'

It was almost midnight. Abu Fahd's exultation increased, for he had drunk three glasses of arak. Again he burst out drunkenly:

'Poor me, what a state I'm in!'

It seemed to him that his raucous voice was filled with an exquisite sweetness and he told himself aloud: 'I'm in fine voice.'

He imagined people with mouths agape waving their hands, cheering and clapping. He laughed for a long time, then tilted his tarboosh slightly back. He resumed singing joyfully:

'Poor me, what a state I'm in!'

He was wearing grey-coloured baggy trousers and had an old yellow belt round his waist. When he arrived under the arched bridge where the darkness was stronger than the light, he was surprised to see a small black sheep standing against the wall. He opened his mouth in amazement and said to himself: 'I'm not drunk. Look well, man, what do you see? It's a sheep. Where's its owner?'

He looked about him but found no one – the alley was utterly deserted. Then, staring at the sheep, he said to himself: 'Am I drunk?'

He gave a low laugh and said to himself: 'Allah is Munificent, He knows that Abu Fahd and Umm Fahd haven't eaten meat for a week.' Abu Fahd approached the sheep and tried to force it to move along by pushing it forwards, but it refused to budge. Abu

Fahd therefore seized it by its two small horns and tugged at them, but the sheep remained rigidly against the wall. Abu Fahd regarded it with fury, then said to it:

'I'll carry you off – and your mother and father too.'

Abu Fahd took the sheep and lifted it up and placed it on his back, holding its two front legs in his hands, then proceeded on his way while resuming his singing, his joyous elation much increased. After a while, though, he stopped singing for he was conscious that the sheep had grown in size and weight. All of a sudden he heard a voice saying: 'Let me be.'

Abu Fahd's forehead knotted into a frown and he said to himself: 'May Allah curse drunkenness.'

After some moments he heard the same voice saying: 'Let me be, I'm not a sheep.'

Abu Fahd shuddered and his terror impelled him to hold fast to the sheep. He came to a halt and the voice spoke again:

'I'm the son of the King of the Djinn. Let me be and I'll give you anything you want.'

Abu Fahd didn't reply but continued on his way with hasty steps.

'I'll give you seven jars filled with gold.'

Abu Fahd imagined he heard the ring of pieces of gold dropping down from some nearby place and striking the ground.

The sheep slipped from him, and he turned around just as he had been about to say: 'Let's have them.'

He found himself alone in the long narrow alley. He couldn't find the sheep and remained nailed to the spot for a while in terror, then continued hastily on his way. On arriving home he woke up his wife Umm Fahd and told her of what had happened.

'Go to sleep, you're drunk,' she said.

'I only had three glasses.'

'You get dizzy on a single glass.'

Abu Fahd felt he'd been insulted, so he answered defiantly:

'I don't get dizzy on a whole barrel of arak.'

Umm Fahd uttered not a word and began bringing to mind the tales she'd heard as a child about the djinn and their sport.

Abu Fahd undressed, switched off the light and stretched out beside his wife, pulling the coverlet up to his chin.

Suddenly Umm Fahd said:

'You should not have let it go before it'd given you the gold.'

Abu Fahd did not answer and Umm Fahd continued with fervour:

'Go tomorrow and take hold of it and don't let it go.'

Abu Fahd gave a tired, sad yawn.

'And how shall I find it?' he asked wearily.

'For certain you'll find it under the bridge. Bring it home and we won't let it go till it gives us the money.'

'I won't find it.'

'The djinn live by day under the ground. When night comes they go up to the earth's surface and sport there till dawn draws near. If they have come to like a particular place, they continually return to it. You will find the sheep under the bridge.'

Abu Fahd stretched out his hand to her bosom and thrust it between her breasts, where he left it motionless.

'We'll become rich,' he said.

'We'll buy a house.'

'A house with a garden.'

'And we'll buy a radio.'

'A large one.'

'And a washing machine.'

'A washing machine.'

'We won't eat any more crushed wheat.'

'We'll eat white bread.'

Umm Fahd laughed like a child, while Abu Fahd continued: 'I'll buy you a red dress.'

'Just one dress?' whispered Umm Fahd in a tone of reproof.

'I'll buy you a hundred dresses.'

Abu Fahd was silent for several moments, then enquired:

'When will you give birth?'

'In three months.'

'It'll be a boy.'

'He'll not suffer as we did.'

'He won't go hungry.'

'His clothes will be beautiful and clean.'

'He won't have to search around for work.'

'He'll study at schools.'

'The owner of the house won't ask him for rent.'

'He'll be a doctor when he grows up.'

'I want him to be a lawyer.'

'We'll ask him: Do you want to be a lawyer or a doctor?'

She clung to him tenderly and continued by enquiring in a sly tone:

'And won't you marry again?'

He gave her ear a light nip:

'Why should I marry? You're the best woman on earth.'

They lapsed into silence, being immersed in a great, tranquil feeling of elation.

But after a while Abu Fahd took away the coverlet from his body with a sudden movement.

'What's wrong?' asked Umm Fahd.

'I'll go now.'

'Where to?'

'I'll bring the sheep.'

'Wait till tomorrow night. Sleep now.'

He hurriedly left the bed, switched on the light that hung from the ceiling and began dressing.

'Maybe you won't find it.'

'I'll find it.'

'Be careful not to let it go,' said Umm Fahd as she helped him wrap the yellow belt round his waist.

Abu Fahd felt that he was venturing upon some hazardous undertaking. He would be in need of his dagger, a dagger with embossed blade and swarthy gleam.

Leaving the house and setting off at speed till he arrived under the bridge, he was overcome by a sense of frustration when he didn't find the sheep. The alley was vacant, and the windows of the houses scattered along the two sides had their lights switched off.

Abu Fahd stood waiting, motionless, resting his back against the wall. After a while there came to his ears a noise that drew closer and presently there appeared a drunken man who was staggering and bumping against the walls of the alley, while he shouted in a drawn-out voice:

'Hey, I'm a man.'

On drawing near Abu Fahd, the man came to a stop and stared in utter astonishment.

'What are you doing here?' he said in a stumbling, joyful voice.

'Get out.'

The drunken man knotted his brows in thought, then his face became radiant with joy:

'By Allah, I too love women. Are you waiting for the husband to go to sleep and for the wife to open the door to you?'

Abu Fahd was annoyed; he felt his irritation growing within him as the drunken man continued what he had to say:

'Is the woman beautiful?'

'What woman?' said Abu Fahd with exasperation.

'The woman you're waiting for.'

'Get out.'

'I'll be your partner.'

Abu Fahd's anger grew more intense, for he feared that the sheep would not make an appearance because of the drunken man's presence.

'Get on your way or I'll break your head,' he said fiercely.

The drunken man belched. 'Are you ordering me about?' he said in a tone of surprise. 'Who do you think you are?'

He was silent for a while, then added: 'Come and break my head. Come on.'

'Go away and leave me,' said Abu Fahd. 'I don't want to break your head.'

'No, no,' said the drunken man indignantly. 'Come along and break my head.'

He backed away slightly and said in a joyful voice:

'I'll turn you into a sieve.'

The drunken man plunged his hand into his trouser pocket and extracted from it a long-bladed razor. Abu Fahd put his hand to his belt, unsheathing his dagger, while the drunken man approached him warily yet with speed.

Abu Fahd raised his dagger high and brought it down, at which the drunken man moved to the left with lightning suddenness so that the dagger didn't touch him, and thrust the razor into Abu Fahd's chest as he shouted: 'Take that!'

Withdrawing the razor from the flesh, the man backed away slightly. Abu Fahd clung closely to the mud wall and raised his dagger a second time, but the drunken man's razor again stabbed him in the chest. The third time he was stabbed in the right shoulder and at once his arm dangled limply and the fingers released the dagger, which fell to the ground.

Leaping about around him, the drunk man shouted:

'Take this . . . and this.'

He stabbed him in the waist. Abu Fahd gave a moan and his knees went weak. He tried to remain standing steadily on his feet, but the razor was launching attacks at him, striking his flesh and tearing it without relaxation.

'Take that,' shouted the drunken man.

He stabbed Abu Fahd in the stomach and his entrails spilled out. Abu Fahd pressed his hands against them: they were hot, wet and quivering. He slipped and fell down. He lay sprawled on his back, while the drunken man, standing close by him, leaned over, coughed several times, vomited, then ran off.

Abu Fahd heard the sheep say to him:

'Seven jars of gold.'

Much gold fell down, glittering like a small sun. Then the sound of it began to move ever further and further away.

GHASSAN KANAFANI

The Slave Fort

Had he not been so sadly shabby one would have said of him that he was a poet. The site he had chosen for his humble hut of wood and beaten-out jerry cans was truly magnificent; right by the threshold the might of the sea flowed under the feet of the sharp rocks with a deep-throated, unvarying sound. His face was gaunt, his beard white though streaked with a few black hairs, his eyes hollow under bushy brows; his cheekbones protruded like two rocks that had come to rest either side of the large projection that was his nose.

Why had we gone to that place? I don't remember now. In our small car we had followed a rough, miry and featureless road. We had been going for more than three hours when Thabit pointed through the window and gave a piercing shout:

'There's the Slave Fort.'

This Slave Fort was a large rock the base of which had been eaten away by the waves so that it resembled the wing of a giant bird, its head curled in the sand, its wing outstretched above the clamour of the sea.

'Why did they call it "The Slave Fort"?'

'I don't know. Perhaps there was some historical incident which gave it the name. Do you see that hut?'

And once again Thabit pointed, this time towards the small hut lying in the shadow of the gigantic rock. He turned off the engine and we got out of the car.

'They say that a half-mad old man lives in it.'

'What does he do with himself in this waste on his own?'

'What any half-mad old man would do.'

From afar we saw the old man squatting on his heels at the entrance to his hut, his head clasped in his hands, staring out to sea.

'Don't you think there must be some special story about this old man? Why do you insist he's half-mad?'

'I don't know, that's what I heard.'

Thabit, having arrived at the spot of his choice, levelled the sand, threw down the bottles of water, took out the food from the bag, and seated himself.

'They say he was the father of four boys who struck it lucky and are now among the richest people in the district.'

'And then?'

'The sons quarrelled about who should provide a home for the father. Each wife wanted her own way in the matter and the whole thing ended with the old man making his escape and settling down here.'

'It's a common enough story and shouldn't have turned the old man half-mad.'

Thabit looked at me uncomprehendingly, then lit the small heap of wood he had arranged, and poured water into the metal water-jug and set it on the fire.

'The important thing in the story is to agree about whether his flight was a product of his mad half or his sane half.'

'There he is, only a few yards away – why not go over and ask him?'

Thabit blew at the fire, then began rubbing his eyes as he sat up straight, resting his body on his knees.

'I can't bear the idea which the sight of him awakens in me.'

'What idea?'

'That the man should spend seventy years of his life so austerely, that he should work, exert himself, existing day after day and hour after hour, that for seventy long years he should gain his daily bread from the sweat of his brow, that he should live through his day in the hope of a better tomorrow, that for seventy whole years he should go to sleep each night – and for what? So that he should, at the last, spend the rest of his life cast out like a dog, alone, sitting like this. Look at him – he's like some polar animal that has lost its fur. Can you believe that a man can live seventy years to attain to this? I can't stomach it.'

Once again he stared at us; then, spreading out the palms of his hands, he continued his tirade:

'Just imagine! Seventy useless, meaningless years. Imagine

walking for seventy years along the same road; the same directions, the same boundaries, the same horizons, the same everything. It's unbearable!'

'No doubt the old man would differ with you in your point of view. Maybe he believes that he has reached an end which is distinct from his life. Maybe he wanted just such an end. Why not ask him?'

We got up to go to him. When we came to where he was he raised his eyes, coldly returned our greeting and invited us to sit down. Through the half-open door we could see the inside of the hut; the threadbare mattress in one corner, while in the opposite one was a square rock on which lay a heap of unopened oyster shells. For a while silence reigned; it was then broken by the old man's feeble voice asking:

'Do you want oyster shells? I sell oyster shells.'

As we had no reply to make to him, Thabit enquired:

'Do you find them yourself?'

'I wait for low tide so as to look for them far out. I gather them up and sell them to those who hope to find pearls in them.'

We stared at each other. Presently Thabit put the question that had been exercising all our minds:

'Why don't you yourself try to find pearls inside these shells?'

'I?'

He uttered the word as though becoming aware for the first time that he actually existed, or as though the idea had never previously occurred to him. He then shook his head and kept his silence.

'How much do you sell a heap for?'

'Cheaply – for a loaf or two.'

'They're small shells and certainly won't contain pearls.'

The old man looked at us with lustreless eyes under bushy brows.

'What do you know about shells?' he demanded sharply. 'Who's to tell whether or not you'll find a pearl?' and as though afraid that if he were to be carried away still further he might lose the deal, he relapsed into silence.

'And can you tell?'

'No, no one can tell,' and he began toying with a shell which lay in front of him, pretending to be unaware of our presence.

166

'All right, we'll buy a heap.'

The old man turned round and pointed to the heap arrayed on the square rock.

'Bring two loaves,' he said, a concealed ring of joy in his voice, 'and you can take that heap.'

On returning to our place bearing the heap of shells, our argument broke out afresh.

'I consider those eyes can only be those of a madman. If not, why doesn't he open the shells himself in the hope of finding some pearls?'

'Perhaps he's fed up with trying and prefers to turn spectator and make money.'

It took us half the day before we had opened all the shells. We piled the gelatinous insides of the empty shells around us, then burst into laughter at our madness.

In the afternoon Thabit suggested to me that I should take a cup of strong tea to the old man in the hope that it might bring a little joy to his heart.

As I was on my way over to him a slight feeling of fear stirred within me. However, he invited me to sit down and began sipping at his tea with relish.

'Did you find anything in the shells?'

'No, we found nothing – you fooled us.'

He shook his head sadly and took another sip.

'To the extent of two loaves!' he said, as though talking to himself, and once again shook his head. Then, suddenly, he glanced at me and explained sharply:

'Were these shells your life – I mean, were each shell to represent a year of your life and you opened them one by one and found them empty, would you have been as sad as you are about losing a couple of loaves?'

He began to shake all over and at that moment I was convinced that I was in the presence of someone who certainly was mad. His eyes, under their bushy brows, gave out a sharp and unnatural brightness, while the dust from his ragged clothes played in the afternoon sun. I could find not a word to say. When I attempted to rise to my feet he took hold of my wrist and his frail hand was strong and convulsive. Then I heard him say:

'Don't be afraid – I am not mad, as you believe. Sit down, I want to tell you something: the happiest moments of my day are when I can watch disappointment of this kind.'

I reseated myself, feeling somewhat calmer.

In the meantime, he began to gaze out at the horizon, seemingly unaware of my presence, as though he had not, a moment ago, invited me to sit down. Then he turned to me.

'I knew you wouldn't find anything. These oysters are still young and therefore can't contain the seed of a pearl. I wanted to know, though.'

Again he was silent and stared out to sea. Then, as though speaking to himself, he said:

'The ebb tide will start early tonight and I must be off to gather shells. Tomorrow other men will be coming.'

Overcome by bewilderment, I rose to my feet. The Slave Fort stood out darkly against the light of the setting sun. My friends were drinking tea around the heaps of empty shells as the old man began running after the receding water, bending down from time to time to pick up the shells left behind.

MAHMOUD AL-WARDANI

The Kerosene Stove

I placed the dark blue teapot with the wooden handle on the yellow tray with the battered edges and went along the corridor, then turned off by the basin, raising the curtain with my elbow and grasping the tray with my right hand alone. I could feel the tray, for its temperature had begun to rise. I pushed the door with my left hand as I slipped my body through, then once again thrust the door to behind me.

I took off my slippers and crossed the carpet barefoot. Uncle Fouad was sitting on the large yellow cushion, leaning against the bed that was covered with a white sheet edged with small blue flowers. He was wearing the mouse-coloured dressing-gown with the squares and a black skull-cap. In front of him was the small brazier on which the heaped embers of coal glowed dully orange, also the large *narghile* with the dark red mouthpiece. He raised his head to me – I used to love him – and stretched out both hands together, taking the tray from me. I crossed by the cylindrical kerosene stove which cast the shadows of its round cover decorated with circles that grew gradually smaller and incorporated within itself and on its edges thousands of small shapes – it cast these shadows of itself on to the ceiling, which they covered completely and which began to be diffracted on the walls where a faint light was shed from the small white shade on the tallboy to the right of Uncle Fouad. I too drew up a small cushion and sat alongside him. 'The concert started some time ago, Uncle Fouad,' I said. 'Yea,' he said. He stretched out his hand to the chair beside the tallboy on which were placed the packets of medicines and the cup in which he kept his false teeth, also the snow-white ashtray – just where the huge, brown-coloured wireless set crouched, with its two white knobs, one each side, looking like human eyes. It wasn't long before the sound came through faintly: Uncle Fouad liked the volume to be like this although recently he had no longer been hearing well. In the mornings, when listening to the news, he would draw up a chair and sit alongside it in the drawing-room by the sideboard. It was always like this with the wireless. Only on the evenings when Umm Kulthoum was giving a concert would he take it inside. It was now that I became aware of the smell that had grown stronger. Uncle Fouad had placed a piece of tangerine peel on top of the stove. The smell was really beautiful; I delighted in it as it became gradually diffused.

'Where's Safiyya?' said Uncle Fouad. 'My Auntie sent her to buy Pepsi,' I said. 'Auntie Kadriyya and Auntie Umm Kamal are in the parlour. Anything you want, Uncle Fouad?' 'That's fine – when she comes,' he said. Now the announcer was talking and I didn't hear him well because he was speaking against a low noise of voices of people presently attending the show at the Kasr El-Nil Cinema. 'Do you know,' said Uncle Fouad, 'that I've related none of this, not even to your brother . . .' He was referring to my elder brother Abdul Azeem who was living with us before moving into the boarding school of music at Helwan two years ago. He said that this place Helwan had a spring that was like the sea, though it wasn't so big you couldn't see anything beyond it. Westerners used to bathe there. Although he would come every two weeks, for he would spend a week with Mother who lived in Shobra with my sister Muna and the following week with us, he no longer used to sit very much, as I did, with Uncle Fouad. This is because he used to take Uncle Fouad's bicycle after we'd leave the mosque on a Friday and go on playing about on it till sunset prayers, which would greatly upset my aunt.

Uncle Fouad began blowing at the coal and the fine white ash flew about and that faint orange glow made its appearance. With his right hand he'd grip the tongs and with his left the bowl of the *narghile*; then he'd put the bowl to one side, also the tongs, and bite off a bit from the dark brown piece he had unwrapped from its cellophane. He put into place a small piece the size of a lentil grain. When I had grown up and entered my pre-university studies, and Uncle Fouad was no longer able to go out very much because of his rheumatism which had of late got much worse, I would take the money to 'Uncle' Antar, a man with one arm who was married to two women who were continually at war with him in those rooms behind the railway station and which would be inhabited by vendors of vegetables, of roasted corn cobs and of newspapers. I used to say to 'Uncle' Antar that Uncle Fouad sends his regards, and he would say 'God bless you,' and he'd disappear over there behind the trees at the far end of the enclosure. When I couldn't find him I'd go to Umm Mahmoud at the grocer's shop beside the church. I'd then come back and say nothing to my aunt.

Uncle Fouad went on inhaling and the small pieces of coal on the bowl on top of the *narghile* gave off slight flickers, while the water began gurgling behind the glass that was decorated with green and golden circles, and he would expel the dense, cohesive smoke from both his nose and mouth. When he had finished he would cough so violently that I'd think he'd dislocate his chest. 'Your father,' said Uncle Fouad, 'hadn't yet married your mother and I hadn't married your aunt – ' he was the son of both Father's paternal uncle and maternal aunt. 'In those days we had taken our degree and had been appointed to posts in the same month. My father, God rest his soul, had bought two suits: a suit for your father and a suit for me, and a tarboosh for your father and a tarboosh for me. Anyway, the fact was it was late and we couldn't find any transport. We were still living, the whole of the family, in the Al-Gharbaleen house. We decided, your father and I, that we'd walk it – in those days we were of course in our youth. We found at your Uncle Fikry's place – he who was newly married and lived in Zeytoun – some French Courvoisier.' Uncle Fouad turned to me: he was smiling and those long lines that ran down from his eyes had completely relaxed. I used to love him when he laughed like this. 'Ah, in those days we used to drink, and I only gave it up before the marriage of "the greatly lamented" ' – the 'greatly lamented' being my Aunt Fayza, the daughter of my Uncle Fikry, who was brought up by Uncle Fouad and my aunt because they hadn't had any children. She had died after giving birth to fair-complexioned Fatin, who was now grown up – three years my junior – and lived with my Uncle Fikry in Zeytoun. 'Anyway, the fact was,' said Uncle Fouad, 'we had drunk a lot, and we went on walking and talking near the

King's Palace in Kubba. Near the entrance we found the King himself: he was standing having a pee and round him were many men and women laughing loudly.' Then he opened the tallboy and brought out two glasses adorned in faded colours, with the colour of the glass itself verging to a deep yellow. He raised his hand high, grasping the wooden handle of the teapot, and proceeded to pour. I didn't see the dark thread that spouted from the mouth of the teapot and which began making froth and bubbles that burst one after the other. He stretched his hand with the glass to me, and took out the handkerchief from his dressing-gown pocket and began wiping his spectacles, his eyes slightly closed. However, his good eye, which was towards me, was quivering, and from afar there reached my ears the sound of the train coming from the direction of Al-Marg, preceded by the long disjointed shriek of the whistle. It wasn't possible for me to hear the first part of the concert which had in fact started. Then Uncle Fouad began preparing another bowl for the *narghile*. His lips were pursed as he leaned over and blew gently at the coals, which showed a fiery glow the colour of amber. Meanwhile I was extremely happy, breathing in the fragrant smell of the tangerine peel burning on top of the kerosene stove.

I began looking at the three pictures hanging on the wall above the chair and facing the chiffonier. The picture in the middle showed Uncle Fouad standing, not wearing his glasses, and my aunt sitting dressed in her wedding clothes and carrying a few flowers, which she clutched to her breast; her feet were pressed together and she was laughing. As for the picture to the right of Uncle Fouad and my aunt, it showed my Uncle Fikry and Auntie Fathiyya when they were being married; Auntie Fathiyya, though, wasn't carrying any flowers. The picture to the left of that of Uncle Fouad and my aunt was of my Aunt Aliyya and my Uncle Abbas; they were standing and his hand was stretched out and placed on her shoulder. She was laughing and looking at him. Then once again came the sound of the wireless – it was Umm Kulthoum singing 'That's What Love's Like', which we'd heard in the previous concert. 'In a second,' said Uncle Fouad, 'we had sobered up from all we had drunk. We began to shake as he turned to us while peeing. Then he shouted –' 'The king?' said I. 'Yes,' he said, 'the King shouted: "Hey, you sons of bitches, what are you two walking along by the Palace for?" He turned to a man beside him and screamed: "The pistol." We told ourselves that we were going to die and I myself muttered: "I bear witness that there is no god but God and that Muhammad is His Prophet." One of the ladies had approached him and said: "Let Your Majesty forgive them," and she stretched out her bare arm and grasped his. I was able to see the side of his face and his full moustache. Then she began whispering in his ear, at which the King laughed loudly and screamed at us: "Get out of my sight, the two of you, you sons of bitches." We ran off and his voice as he laughed was still carried to us by the wind, until we got to Kubba Bridge.' I looked at Uncle Fouad and he too was laughing. He said: 'Let's hear the rest of the concert.'

After a while I heard the sound of the door of the flat. 'Safiyya's come,' I said. 'I'll call her, Uncle Fouad.' I got up and put on my slippers, then closed the door behind me. It was slightly cold in the parlour and their voices – those of our women neighbours – came to me from the drawing-room blended with that of my aunt who was laughing.